"Maybe it's time be kissed again."

Gina stared at Connor, her body as rigid as if she'd been hypnotized. Her breath felt frozen within her lungs.

He kept his eyes trained on hers. "You're very kissable, Gina. Very desirable. But you remind me of a princess in a fairy tale. A spell's been cast on you. And you lie caught in that spell, protected by your fortress. This town is your fortress."

She reached deep inside herself for words. "This town—"

"Shh," he said. "Listen. Just a moment longer. In the stories, the spell can be broken by a kiss. Not just any kiss—the *right* kiss."

Dear Reader,

Arkansas's *real* spaghetti feast—and a true feast it is—is put on by the women of St. Joseph's Church in Tontitown during the town's annual Grape Festival. True Tontitown spaghetti has no spices other than salt and pepper. The secret is in the sauce's incredible richness.

Cathy Ardemagni's spaghetti is held in reverence by all who have been lucky enough to taste it at one of the annual dinners. This is her personal recipe. It's *large*—the recipe makes five gallons—because her children and her friends always beg for a supply. It can be frozen.

CATHY ARDEMAGNI'S SPAGHETTI SAUCE
1 lb ground salt pork
1 lb ground fresh garlic
5-7 medium onions, chopped
10-12 lbs lean ground round steak
5 lbs finely ground chicken gizzards (optional)
2 64 oz cans tomato paste
4 64 oz cans tomato puree
1 lb butter
salt and pepper to taste
1 lb whole peeled carrots (Remove after cooking. The carrots cut the acidity of the tomatoes.)

Sauté salt pork until it starts to brown. Add garlic, then onions, and continue to sauté until brown. Add ground round steak, stir until seared. Add gizzards and stir until seared.

Stir in tomato puree and paste. You may need to add water to thin. Bring to a good simmer, add butter, salt, pepper and carrots. Turn sauce to low heat. Continue to stir frequently. Cook for six hours.

Serve over spaghetti and garnish with freshly ground Parmesan cheese.

The Tontitown Grape Festival takes place during the week of the Feast of the Annunciation, often the second week in August. Carnival runs until midnight with midway rides, arts and crafts booths and live music. The women of the church make and package extra pasta, so you can even take some home with you. Italian spaghetti dinners are served from 4:30 to 8:30 p.m. at the St. Joseph's Church parish hall.

Y'all come—but be prepared to stand in line!

Sincerely,

Bethany Campbell

P.S. If you think every good meal should end with dessert, don't miss Earline's Brownie recipe following this story!

ADD A LITTLE SPICE
Bethany Campbell

Harlequin Books

TORONTO • NEW YORK • LONDON
AMSTERDAM • PARIS • SYDNEY • HAMBURG
STOCKHOLM • ATHENS • TOKYO • MILAN
MADRID • WARSAW • BUDAPEST • AUCKLAND

To Cathy Ardemagni

ISBN 0-373-03260-9

Harlequin Romance first edition April 1993

ADD A LITTLE SPICE

Printed in U.S.A.

CHAPTER ONE

IT WAS FESTIVAL TIME in the little town of Allegro, Arkansas. That meant, as usual, the house was full of elephants, each of them dressed differently.

There was an elephant, almost two feet tall, in a white tutu and ballet slippers, another in a scarlet dress with a hoop skirt, a third in farmer's overalls. One elephant wore a turban and robe, another a diamond tiara and ball gown of blue silk.

Gina Calvino and her great-aunt Earline were wrapping the stuffed animals in tissue paper to take to the craft fair. All year long Earline sewed the dolls and their costumes. She was a true artist of elephants, and like all artists, temperamental. The nearer the festival and craft fair drew, the more temperamental she became.

"I hate this," Earline grumbled. Sixty years old, she was small, round and excitable, with bright black eyes and snow-white curls. Her mood for the day was contentious. "Every year it's worse—a circus. Bah. Next year I'm going to lock the doors and stay inside until it's over."

"Ha," Gina laughed, bundling up an elephant dressed like an angel. Gina took Earline's changes in mood as naturally as she took changes in the weather. The older woman had practically raised her.

"Ha, yourself," Earline muttered, energetically rustling tissue paper. "The festival's gotten too big. And the town's dying, anyway. All good things must end. I'm a realist."

Gina shook her head in amiable disagreement, knowing Earline didn't mean it. "The festival should go on forever," she said. "The town, too." A tall young woman of twenty-five, Gina had a mass of unruly, shoulder-length auburn curls. She laughed quickly, and she laughed often, although sometimes one could detect sadness hiding deep within her dark eyes. Her smile, especially when her dimples played, was her greatest beauty. Her dimples showed now.

"Nothing goes on forever," Earline countered. "Why a tomato festival? Hardly anybody farms tomatoes anymore. All the young people leave Allegro to find jobs. Someday this town will vanish—poof."

Gina's dimples disappeared. "No." Her voice became soft, almost solemn. "That's why we *have* the festival. It keeps us a community."

Earline straightened, rubbing her back and looking resigned. For forty years she had worked as the secretary of the local grade school. But next spring the school would close its doors forever. The students would be bused instead to the neighboring town of Milledgeville, six miles away. Earline, always the fatalist, took it as a sign that Allegro's end was nigh.

"To everything there is a season," Earline said, squaring her shoulders. "Face it—the festival's too big for us now. *Finita la commedia.* The game is up."

"The festival's successful," Gina said with equanimity, "that's all."

"There's such a thing as too much success. The work— the crowds—the fuss—the traffic—and the *dust*—ack! And the whole town filled with strangers."

"But it's homecoming time, too," Gina said, tucking the angel into the box that held its cousins. "It's when people come back to visit."

Earline was silent a moment, but her black eyes grew somber. "Right," she said cynically, reaching for another elephant. "But nobody's coming back to us."

Gina lowered her head, avoiding her aunt's gaze. What was left of their family had scattered so far that nobody returned to Allegro these days. Only Earline and Gina were there.

"You should get married, have a family," Earline said abruptly. "Our line's dying out—just like the town."

Gina said nothing and pretended to concentrate on opening another package of tissue paper.

"You've mourned long enough," Earline said. "It's time to get on with your life."

Gina, acting unconcerned, shrugged. "I'm not mourning. I am getting on with my life. It's festival, and I've got a thousand things to do."

"Bah!" Earline said with vehemence. She looked at her great-niece critically, from head to toe. "You're going to wear *that* all day?"

Gina wore faded jeans and an enormous red T-shirt that said, "Allegro Tomato Festival—99 Glorious Years!" She had on tattered running shoes, but no socks.

Her only adornment was the antique Mickey Mouse watch she always wore. And, of course, her engagement ring with its tiny diamond. She never took off the ring.

"I troubleshoot today," she said airily. "I may have to crawl under the merry-go-round to rescue a cat, or haul a case of salt into the kitchen. Why dress up?"

Earline tilted her chin stubbornly. "To give somebody a chance to notice what a pretty girl you are."

"I'm not in a beauty contest. I have to work." Gina picked up an elephant dressed like a red devil and began to wrap it.

"It's a sin the way you live in the past," Earline said with sudden passion. "It's gone on too long. It's not right."

Gina bit her lower lip and tucked the devil's horns safely inside the tissue. Memories swarmed through her mind like a pack of unruly ghosts.

Loren, her fiancé, had died five years ago this summer. She had loved Loren with all her being, and he'd loved her. They were to be married that September and would live in Allegro, as they had done all their lives. Loren would coach high school football in neighboring Milledgeville, and Gina would open a little antique shop, just as she'd always dreamed. She had also inherited a small spice business from her father that she would run in her spare time.

That last summer, before he was to start his coaching job, Loren had worked for the electric company as a lineman. One stormy August night he was dispatched to repair a power line between Allegro and Milledgeville. The man who went with Loren said that Loren was near the top of a pole, the rain driving around him. He reached his arm straight over his head toward an insulator, when suddenly lightning turned the night sky a blinding white.

For a moment Loren's body had arced in agony against the blazing sky as white-hot sparks danced around his outstretched hand. Then he sagged, lifeless, kept from falling to earth only by his safety belt.

Solemn men came to her door in the darkness and rain to tell her. Loren, twenty-two years old, strong and handsome and serious and sweet, was dead. Loren, who in three weeks would have been her husband.

After the funeral, Gina locked herself in her room, and there she stayed. Earline, concerned, would knock and try to talk to her, and finally she started leaving trays of food by the door. Gina barely answered. Sometimes she would eat, and sometimes she would not. All she thought of was Loren.

Once, in a somber moment, he had said that if anything ever happened to him, he hoped Gina would not change. He hoped she would always be his happy, laughing, high-

spirited Gina. Would she promise him that? She had promised.

For three weeks she grieved for him, deeply and pri-
vately. On the day that was to have been their wedding day,
she came out of her room, pale but smiling, and seeming
almost like her old self. The townspeople were amazed at her
resilience.

Gina's smile had been for Loren. When she'd walked out
of her room that day, she walked to the wedding march. She
felt as if she were making her vows to Loren and making
them forever. She would laugh and be her old self. But she
would also be faithful to his memory. Always.

"Gina, don't go off into a dreamworld," Earline said. "I
mean it. I know you *seem* happy. But it's time you really
were happy again."

"You're imagining things," Gina said lightly. She finished wrapping the devil and put it into the box with the
other elephants.

"No, I'm not." Earline put her hand on her hip and
stared at Gina with a mixture of affection and concern.
"You should find a nice man. Everybody thinks you're going to become an old eccentric. You should show them."

Gina picked up another elephant. "I don't have to show
anybody anything. I'm fine."

Earline reached out and gently raised Gina's chin so that
their eyes met. "You need more in life than throwing yourself into every town project. More than just the antique shop
and the spice garden and this old house and me."

Gina took her aunt's hand and smiled, her dimples reap-
pearing. "Earline, I don't want a man. I inherited you from
Mama's side and the spices from Daddy's. I've got my shop,
the museum, the festival—I love it all. I love the whole
town. You never got married. Why should I?"

Earline's chin quivered, but her eyes snapped dark fire.
"How can a woman be happy only loving a town? Look at
you. You're so thin. No meat on you at all."

"You're just jealous." Gina laughed. "You dream of being thin again—right?"

For emphasis, Gina backed up against Earline and bumped her slender bottom against Earline's well-padded one. Earline tried to scowl. "Don't change the subject—and don't be so...so..." She searched for a word.

"Cheeky?" Gina teased, and bumped bottoms again.

Earline ignored the joke. "You get stranger every year," she grumbled. "You're getting very odd, Gina."

"Hey," Gina said with a grin, "at least I don't spend my time dressing elephants, do I?" And she laughed again because she'd meant what she'd said. She was no longer in mourning—at least, hardly at all—and she loved the town as if it were husband, children, and home all rolled into one.

THAT EVENING Gina looked at the cars jamming the narrow highway into town. The setting sun glinted on hundreds of them, the line of vehicles stretching as far as the eye could see.

The madness begins in earnest now, she thought, and her heartbeat quickened.

Tonight was the first night of the annual Tomato Festival in Allegro. Carnival lights gleamed through the August dusk, and the Ferris wheel, slowly turning, rose like an enchanted beacon above all else.

The entire celebration seemed in fine form—and bigger than ever. Too big, a few disgruntled townspeople thought; but they were in a minority. Still there was no denying it: for the next three days, life in Allegro would be topsy-turvy.

Like most townspeople, Gina didn't mind. The more the festival sprawled, the better. All the planning, the hard work, even the confusion, made her blood sing. *The whole town works together,* she thought with a surge of pride and wonder. *Together, we make this magic.*

Magic it was. On the midway, the merry-go-round horses pranced, the tilt-a-whirl spun, the bumper cars collided, the rollo-planes rose and plunged as riders screamed in terror or whooped with laughter. Barkers hawked their games to passersby.

Across the street, dozens of arts-and-crafts booths displayed their colorful wares: handmade dolls, paintings, homemade jellies and jams and tomato preserves, turquoise jewelry, wood carvings, afghans and quilts. And, of course, Earline's costumed elephants.

Outside the parish hall, twin lines of people stretched almost three blocks down the sidewalks, impatient for the dinners served there. Allegro was famous throughout the state for its delicious spaghetti suppers, cooked by the women of the church.

Each year Gina helped mix, cut and dry the hundreds of pounds of pasta eaten at the festival. She worked days ahead to help cook the gallons and gallons of sauce. Now its spicy fragrance wafted deliciously over the festival grounds. Mingled with it were the midway aromas of popcorn, taffy apples and cotton candy.

The doors to the hall had opened, and the parish women had started ladling out the fabled spaghetti. Outside, the hungry crowd shifted restlessly, for the hall would only seat three hundred at a time, and each night thousands came, waiting their turn at the feast.

Gina wholeheartedly loved the festival. It was not only a celebration of the harvest, but of the town's proud Italian heritage. For ninety-nine years, the festival had symbolized the unique spirit of Allegro and its people.

And, for ninety-nine years, Gina's family had been an integral part of the festival. It was her great-great-grandmother's spice combination that was used in the spaghetti sauce, giving it its inimitable aroma and flavor. For four generations, the family had grown and shared the spices—but never their secret. Gina supposed that she would leave the recipe to the church when she was gone. She would have no children to pass it on to.

When she thought of that, the sparkle faded from her eyes. She and Loren would have started a family by now, and his parents would still be living in Allegro, celebrating with them. But his parents had left the state after his death. He had been their only son, and they said too many memories made the town unbearable for them. There were no children for Gina. There never would be.

Gina couldn't help it; each year when the festival started, she felt a lump in her throat like a stone. Loren had loved this time of year. Since childhood they had celebrated the festival together, laughing at the madness it engendered. That's what she remembered best about Loren, how serious he was, but how she could always make him laugh.

She stared up at the Ferris wheel and bit her lip. For this year's festival, she had volunteered to be a troubleshooter. She was supposed to be carrying change to the ice-cream booth, but when the carnival lights had twinkled on, she had paused to admire them. Now, although the change bag was tucked under her arm and people awaited her, she was still held motionless, as if in a spell.

I should be smiling, she thought. *Loren would want me to smile. I will in a minute. But right now I can't.*

Then, mercifully, someone tapped her shoulder. She turned, grateful for the distraction, and saw Mary Ellen Orsini. Gina could tell by Mary Ellen's expression that trouble was afoot. "Yes?" she asked warily.

Mary Ellen leaned forward conspiratorially and whispered in Gina's ear, "We've got a problem—Billy Ray has gone and busted right out of his pants."

Gina's reverie shattered, and reality charged back to claim her. Billy Ray had split his pants?

She didn't know whether to laugh or to cry. She slapped her forehead in frustration. "I knew it. I *warned* him."

"So did I," Mary Ellen agreed righteously. "Now what?"

Gina tried to think fast. She stepped back, narrowed her eyes and studied Mary Ellen's stocky figure. She squared her shoulders, then leaned and whispered in Mary Ellen's ear.

"Oh, Gina!" Mary Ellen cried, recoiling in horror. "I can't. He won't. He just *won't*."

"Yes, he will," Gina answered, her voice grim, "or he'll answer to *me*. Now hurry, Mary Ellen—please."

"Oh!" cried Mary Ellen. She darted off, weaving through the crowd, talking to herself. "*Never* in the history of the festival, never, never...."

GINA STOOD in the small back room of the parish hall, furiously sewing up the spangled pants belonging to the Elvis impersonator.

Every night the festival rang with music, and that night's special feature was Billy Ray Fenelli, a man who looked like Elvis Presley and did an exceptionally good imitation of him. But since last year, Billy Ray had gained weight. He'd had trouble fastening his Elvis pants, and when he'd tried to sit, the back seam had ripped.

"I went from thin Elvis to fat Elvis in the blink of an eye," Billy Ray mourned. He stood with a flowered towel wrapped around his ample middle while Gina worked as fast as she could to mend the pants.

"Too many jelly doughnuts, Billy Ray," Gina said, needle flashing. "I sent Mary Ellen home for a girdle. You and she are about the same size."

"A girdle?" Billy Ray clutched his flowered towel more tightly, as if it would protect him from this humiliation. "I won't wear no girdle. The *King* don't wear no girdle."

"This king will—unless you want to explode out of your kingly pants again," Gina said, setting her jaw.

"No, I won't."

"Yes, you will—or you can go out and imitate Elvis in that towel. So *there*."

"Dammit, Gina!" Billy Ray wailed. But at last Gina knew she'd won, just as she'd intended. It was known throughout the town that few could stand up to Gina Calvino, especially once she'd made up her mind.

As she left the parish hall, she couldn't help smiling over Billy Ray's predicament. *My life is absurd,* she thought, hurrying down the steps, past all the waiting customers. *But at least it's not dull.*

A fat, bespectacled little boy named Wesley Dean Paris, who lived next door to Earline and her, rushed up from behind and tugged hard at her T-shirt. "Gina! Gina!"

She turned, brushing back her curly bangs. Wesley was such a high-strung child that all of life's events seemed incredibly wild and dramatic to him. "What, Wesley Dean?"

Wesley Dean was so excited he hopped up and down, waving his arms and making a small noise that sounded like *erk.* "Lindy Marchesi—erk—she sent me. You know the popcorn booth?"

"Stop *hopping,* Wesley Dean. You're shaking the steps."

Wesley only hopped harder. "Listen—erk—Lindy just started a new batch of popcorn—and her old boyfriend came by, and he threw a frog in the popper."

Gina seized him by his plump shoulders. "What?" she cried in horror. "A live frog?"

Wesley wriggled and bounced. "Nobody can tell—the corn's popping. Lindy's crying, she's afraid the frog exploded, and she won't touch it. Could you—erk—"

Gina released him and sprinted down the steps, racing for the popcorn booth.

She nearly collided with a lean elderly man, dressed with daunting stylishness in a seersucker suit and white shoes.

"Oomph!" said Gina, when he caught her just before she crashed into him. "Excuse me."

She tried to extricate herself from his grasp, but he was surprisingly strong and held her at arm's length, staring into her face. He had grizzled eyebrows and, despite his genial expression, the coldest blue eyes she'd ever seen.

"Miss Calvino?" he asked, showing white teeth in a smile she instantly disliked. "Miss Gina Calvino?"

"Excuse me," Gina repeated, trying to wriggle away. "I have to check the popfrog—the popcorn."

The old man smiled more widely and gripped her more tightly. "Miss Calvino, I'm told that you're responsible for the taste of that fine spaghetti being served in the hall. That you own the secret of its spices. Is that true?"

Gina stared at him in irritation. The more widely the smile stretched across his wrinkled face, the less she trusted it. "I own a small spice company," she said. "I supply the spices, yes. But I really can't—"

"And I really can't lose this opportunity to compliment you," he interrupted smoothly. "I'm in the food business myself. My name is Morton Beekman. Founder of Dee-Lish Foods."

Gina nodded, still trying to draw away politely. She'd heard that the founder of Dee-Lish Foods—somebody named Beekman—was in Milledgeville, buying a vinegar factory. *Beekman,* she thought uneasily. *Why isn't he tending his vinegar? What's he doing here?*

He bent so close that his skull-like face filled her vision. "I'd like to talk to you—businessman to businesswoman."

"Some other time," she said from between her teeth. She tried to pry his hand from her arm. "I'm busy."

"So am I," Beekman said, not easing his grip. "I won't mince words. I'm interested in buying it—the secret of your spices. Your recipe."

Gina stopped struggling and glowered at him. She didn't like this old man, and she didn't like his offer. For years people had tried to beg, buy or borrow the recipe. Her family's answer had always been *no,* and it always would be.

"It's not for sale, Mr. Beekman. I promised my father it'd never leave the family and it never will. Now please let me go."

"Life's taught me an important rule, Miss Calvino." Beekman grinned, leaning closer still. "Everything has its price. And everyone."

Gina's emotions, already in tumult, flared. "Every rule has exceptions, Mr. Beekman. The recipe isn't for sale. Neither am I." She knocked his hands away with such force that he blinked with surprise.

She bolted off so swiftly that she didn't see Beekman staring after her. His false smile died away, and his mouth became a thin determined line.

"Feisty," Beekman muttered to himself, watching her long legs bear her into the crowd. "Very feisty. The kind it's most fun to break."

Gina sprinted to the popcorn booth, only to find that Lindy's father, Ralph, had already come to the rescue and stopped the popper. The frog proved to be a lifelike rubber one, although it was now slightly melted.

She gave Lindy an encouraging pat on the back, then went on her way. She walked down the midway alone, staring up at the lights.

She gave no further thought to Morton Beekman or his unexpected offer. Instead, she inhaled the familiar scents of the festival, savored its sights and sounds—the bandstand with its live music, the fun house echoing with the shrieks of its patrons, the thronging crowd, and balloons bobbing everywhere.

It's a good life, a fulfilling life, Gina thought, listening to the music of the carousel. *I don't need anything else, now or ever.*

She stopped a moment and held out her left hand, letting the lights play in the facets of her little diamond. Its sparkle seemed to tell her that even if she sometimes felt a twinge of loneliness, she must ignore it.

In her mind she blew Loren a kiss and told him she was still true and always would be.

Then she hid her hand in her pocket and walked on alone.

CHAPTER TWO

IT WAS A BRIGHT BLUE morning in September, two weeks after the festival, that Gina got the first letter from Morton Beekman. She had almost forgotten him.

She and Earline were sitting at the breakfast table, enjoying their coffee. Gina, seeing the name Dee-Lish Foods on the envelope, thought it was some kind of advertisement. But when she opened it and began to read, she frowned.

Dear Ms. Calvino:

My researchers have compiled data on you and your company, on economic projections and the fair worth of your enterprise. I am thus prepared to offer you the sum of five thousand dollars ($5,000) for exclusive rights to Allegro's Old-Fashioned Spaghetti Spices.

Upon completion of this transaction, my lawyers will open negotiations with the town of Allegro in order that Dee-Lish Foods may assume sponsorship of what is now known as the Allegro Tomato Festival.

A dwindling town cannot long continue to manage a festival of such size. Dee-Lish Foods, however, has the means to allow Allegro's tradition to live on in spite of the town's demise.

"Good grief." Gina's voice was slightly strangled.
Slowly Earline raised her eyes. "What is it?"

Gina's face had paled. She thrust the letter toward Earline. "Beekman—the man who talked to me at the festival. He still wants my company. Now he wants to take over the festival, too. Why? What's he thinking of?"

"What?" Earline almost exploded as she scanned the letter. "He's had 'research' done on you? Research? The nerve!"

Gina nodded, troubled. "I have no idea what that means. Has anybody been around asking questions?"

"I don't know," Earline said, militance in her voice. "Beekman's rich. He can probably do it with computers. That's what's going to happen—computers will be the ruin of civilization. I've always said so. And how *dare* he call this a 'dwindling town'? I'd like to dwindle him, the snoop."

Gina stared at her aunt in wary surprise. "But you've been saying the same thing yourself."

Earline's black eyes snapped. "Yes? Well, I *live* here. I can say what I want. But no stranger can insult us...."

Gina crossed her arms on the tablecloth and buried her face in them. She laughed helplessly. "Earline, you're priceless, but imagine—the crazy man wants to buy a *festival*."

"Allegro won't stand for this," Earline snorted. "You're going to tell him no, aren't you?"

Gina, suddenly serious, raised her eyes. "Of course."

"And keep telling him no?"

"Certainly."

"Even if he offers you—" Earline struggled to imagine an unimaginable sum "—fifty thousand dollars?"

Gina shook her head. "Even if he offers a million. I don't sell out my family—or my town."

Earline's eyes suddenly widened. "But, Gina, what if he does? Offer you fifty thousand dollars? What would you do?"

Gina's jaw went steely. "I told you. I would never, never, never sell."

Earline smiled and leaned across the table, patting Gina's hand. "My good girl," she said. "Think! Dee-Lish Foods taking over our festival. What a nightmare."

"It'll never happen. I'll write him this instant." Gina reached over and took Earline's tablet and pen. She clamped her lips together, flipped to a clean page and began writing.

Her cheeks pink with angry determination, Gina scribbled Beekman a terse note. "No," she wrote, "and never raise this matter again. For eternity, the answer is no."

MORTON BEEKMAN would not accept no as an answer, for eternity or otherwise. Every two weeks he sent Gina yet another offer. Each time, she adamantly refused it. The stalemate seemed hopeless. Beekman would not give up. Gina would not give in.

After almost a year, Beekman had grudgingly upped his bid to $30,000. The sum seemed too unreal for Gina even to consider, and it almost began to tempt Earline into changing her mind.

But nearly everyone in Allegro stood behind Gina. The recipe belonged to her family. And the festival belonged to the town by the sacred rite of tradition. No outsider was needed, none was wanted, none would be tolerated.

She must stand firm, people told her, for her honor and for Allegro's. Some things were not meant to be sold.

But as August approached again and the one hundredth annual Allegro Tomato Festival drew near, some citizens suffered nervous twinges. The centennial festival loomed before them as both a challenge and a burden: the biggest, most ambitious and most elaborate festival ever.

Would all the trouble, the traffic, the crowds, the sheer backbreaking labor make some people change their minds? Would they wish the one hundredth festival to be the last?

And what of Beekman? Some began to wonder, darkly, just how much money he might offer in the end. How high would he go? How much would he be willing to pay?

Could Gina keep resisting? She had been remarkably strong so far—and remarkably stubborn.

Still, money was money, and even Gina was only human. So far her conflict with Beekman was classic: irresistible force meets immovable object. Allegro's future would be decided when one surrendered. Eventually, someone must surrender. But who?

THE CAR TRAVELED south on the California Highway beside the Pacific Ocean, which ebbed and surged, almost as dazzling a blue as the sky above.

"Let me get this straight," Connor Munroe said, giving Beekman a lazy sideways glance. "For almost a year you've been hounding this woman in Arkansas? You even set a detective on her?"

Morton Beekman scowled and crushed his hat more tightly onto his head. The two men rode in Connor's convertible, a vehicle Beekman despised. He sank deeper into the seat and scowled on general principle.

"I said," Connor repeated, adjusting his sunglasses, "you set a detective on this poor woman—?"

"I heard you," Morton Beekman snapped. "Don't sound so morally superior. You haven't any right—and don't pass that truck. The road's too narrow."

Connor, cocking a dark blond eyebrow, whipped around the truck anyway, making Beekman cringe. To their right stretched the azure Pacific. To their left, low mountains, velvety with grass, rose toward the jewellike sky. Overhead gulls wheeled, white wings flashing in the sun.

Beekman pulled his hat down more tightly and swore. "Will you ever in your maverick life do the sensible thing?"

Connor laughed. "Probably not." The wind whipped his thick, dark blond hair. "Don't complain. You're the one who wanted to hitch a ride."

"Only because you wouldn't ride in the Rolls. I hate this sardine can." Beekman regarded the interior of the vintage yellow MG with hostility.

"The Rolls is too big," Connor said, draping one wrist over the wheel. "It's like a hearse." He looked up at the sky and inhaled the sea air. Lord, but he liked this stretch of road. If only it didn't lead to Beekman's garlic farm in Salinas Valley. A thousand delights could be found up and down the highway, but Beekman had to be headed for a garlic farm. Typical.

"Watch the road," Beekman ordered. "Do you still really want to buy that fleet of yachts?"

"I suppose." Connor shrugged. He was a tall, broad-shouldered man of thirty-one, bronzed by the sun of both the Mediterranean and California. His hair, longer than was fashionable, was streaked with gold, and he kept his head tilted at a cynical, careless angle.

At the moment, he was a magazine publisher of more than moderate success, but he was growing restless again. For one thing, the magazines were making a healthy profit, and their stable prosperity bored him; it was time to sell them and move on to the next challenge.

For another thing, events of the past year had forced him into unfamiliar inactivity. He was ready for something different, and it might as well be the yachts. He was ready for something new, something demanding.

A year ago he'd mangled his right foot in a waterskiing accident in Spain. Since then, he'd suffered through three operations and months of therapy. He could walk well enough again, but he'd always have a slight limp. The limp slowed him, something he couldn't get used to. He wanted to go adventuring again.

Beekman snorted. "I've got plans of my own for those yachts. The Dee-Lish Gourmet Cruise Fleet. You should stick to what you know. What do you know about a charter business? Go print more magazines."

"I know yachts," Connor said out of the side of his mouth. He'd spent eighteen months on one when he was a child and his mother had been married to old Fred Mercator. Although they'd sailed most of the Caribbean, seldom staying in one place, it had been the most settled time of Connor's life, and the happiest.

Connor had liked Fred Mercator. The old man had seemed like a combination of Santa Claus and an amiable pirate. Mercator's sister, Fanny, often joined them, and Connor had been fond of her, too. Although her hair was graying, she'd had an innocence and vulnerability that made her seem like a child his own age, and she was always a willing playmate.

But then Fred had died, the stricken Fanny had fled back to California, and Connor's mother went on the prowl again. Connor was once more dispatched to a series of boarding schools and summer camps.

Connor had lost track of Mercator's yacht, *The Solitaire*, but he still remembered her, remembered her with something akin to longing.

He'd been trying to track her down for the past five years. Then, this spring, he'd discovered her. She was part of a decrepit Caribbean fleet that had fallen into the hands of Morton Beekman. The irony made him want to gag.

Beekman and Connor were not on cordial terms. Connor's specialty was management, and he literally roamed the world looking for businesses he could salvage. Years ago, Beekman had spotted his talent and tried to hire him. Connor, always fiercely independent, had refused.

Then Beekman applied all the screws at his considerable disposal to force Connor into working for him. It had been an ugly time. Beekman often fought dirty, and Connor resented it. But each man had developed a grudging admiration for the other's toughness.

Beekman was resourceful, Connor had to admit. And he did his homework. Connor had been checked out—just as the woman in Arkansas had. Beekman had discovered Connor had few weaknesses. But he did want to find *The Solitaire*; in fact, he wanted to find her a lot.

The boat, now part of a ramshackle Caribbean charter service, had fallen into Beekman's hands because of a foreclosure. Beekman was planning to transfer all the salvageable boats to the California coast and turn them into floating restaurants.

Connor had come to California to arrange the sale of his chain of travel magazines, the Vagabond Group. Beekman had wasted no time in letting him know he'd gained the prize Connor had wanted for so long: *The Solitaire*.

At first he'd taunted Connor with the fact. He would not consider selling the boat, he said, and Connor knew the refusal rose out of simple spite.

But now, mysteriously, Beekman had agreed to this drive to talk things over. He would think of selling the yacht, he hinted, but only if Connor bought the rest of the shabby fleet, as well. But Beekman was being coy. He was maddening when he was coy.

"You don't know anything about the travel or recreation business," Connor told him. "You're better off selling to me, Morty."

"Don't call me that. It's . . . irreverent."

"I know."

"Bah," said Beekman in disgust. "I've kept track of you. You take chances no sane man would take. Someday your luck'll run out. Then you won't laugh. But I've decided I might sell those boats. *If* the terms are right."

Connor smiled sardonically. Beekman had something up his sleeve all right, and he was about to reveal it at last. "So what are the terms, Morty?"

"I've got something you want—the yachts," Beekman snapped. "You've got nothing I want—anymore. I wouldn't have you on my payroll. You've got too much of a gambler's wild streak. I was crazy to ever think you'd fit into my corporate picture.''

''Fine. So I've got nothing you want. So why are we talking?''

''Because in Arkansas Gina Calvino *does* have something I want. It's simple. Go get me that recipe. I'll sell you the yachts.''

Connor gave Beekman such a long, derisive look that it unnerved the older man. ''Look at the road, look at the road,'' he commanded.

Connor shook his head in amusement and turned his attention back to the highway. ''You're crazy, Morty. Me—go to Arkansas and deal with your muleheaded woman?''

''You want the yachts?'' Beekman said icily. ''You go to Arkansas.''

''Why me? Why should I do any better than you?''

Beekman, still clutching his hat over his ears, sank more grumpily into the MG's bucket seat. ''You have a reputation,'' he said grudgingly. ''You're very... persuasive. The word gets around.'' He paused. ''Besides, I'm not very good with women,'' he admitted. ''You're supposed to be. For what *that's* worth.''

Connor grinned, steering the car around a turn that brought them to a particularly spectacular view of the coastline. Involuntarily he sucked in his breath and his stomach tightened. California would be beautiful, if it weren't for the memories.

Connor's mother had married a Californian a few years after Mercator's death. It was not a happy marriage. Her new husband was no Fred Mercator; he was a bully and a drunk. A rich, mean drunk. Cissie divorced him after two years, but not before he and Connor had clashed too many times to count. Connor's stomach still twisted at the memory.

''Besides,'' Beekman added slyly, giving Connor a sideways look, ''you could make up for that fiasco in San

Francisco. You know—Fred Mercator's sister. This situation is a lot like that one. This time you could get it right.''

Connor's face went taut. He hadn't realized Beekman knew about that, too. Connor wasn't used to failing, but he'd failed badly with Fanny Mercator, and the fact still stung. Connor had few vulnerable spots, but somehow Beekman had found two: first, *The Solitaire;* now, Fanny Mercator.

It had happened years after Fred Mercator's death, when Connor was a grown man. A worried relative, a distant cousin of Fred and Fanny's, had tracked Connor down. The cousin said that Fanny was living as a virtual recluse in a decaying neighborhood in San Francisco.

Connor had been afraid of something like that. As a boy and teenager, he'd tried repeatedly to make contact with her. She'd never answered his letters. Now he learned why.

The relative said she had gone downhill ever since Fred's death. She'd turned into a paranoid old woman, suffering from malnutrition and possibly heart disease. She lived like a pauper although she was hoarding enough computer stock to make her rich. But she wouldn't sell. The stock was her only security, she said, she wouldn't part with it.

Fred had always been able to deal with Fanny's eccentricities, the cousin said. Connor had once been close to the woman. Would he go to San Francisco to reason with Fanny? Would he do it, please, out of respect for Fred's memory and his old affection for Fanny?

Connor went, but from the first he feared he was too late. Fanny Mercator was a tragically changed woman. She was frightened, suspicious and swiftly growing weaker. Yet, for a few fleeting days, he'd thought he'd almost succeeded.

Then, quixotically, her unsteady mind withdrew the small amount of trust she'd bestowed on Connor. She would see him no more, she would speak with him no more.

He started to investigate legal solutions, but before he could get anywhere, she died, alone, neglected and malnourished. She left behind a heap of tattered scrapbooks, a house fit only for demolition and five million dollars in stocks.

"I know all about Fanny Mercator," Beekman said with self-satisfaction. "Now I've got this neurotic spinster in Arkansas, hoarding her spaghetti spices, heading for exactly the same fate."

"I thought she was young," Connor said. His smile had disappeared.

"So was Fanny Mercator—once," Beekman said contemptuously. "I've been after this woman for months. I've offered her everything except the moon. But she won't listen. She lives in a ramshackle old house. With an old great-aunt. The aunt's eccentric, and the Calvino woman's going to be just like her—or worse."

Connor flexed his hands on the wheel and glanced at the surf crashing against the stony coast. The woman in Arkansas did sound somewhat like Fanny Mercator. He didn't like it. "Morty," he said quietly, "you're a rich man. Why even care about a spaghetti sauce?"

Beekman flinched with displeasure. Connor was the only living person with the nerve to call him "Morty."

"I mean," Connor said, his wicked grin returning, "is this the start of your decline? Arkansas's not the spaghetti capital of the universe, you know."

"You're a young fool," Beekman grumbled. "The food business is my life. This spaghetti is the best I've tasted since I was in Bologna—better. Extraordinary stuff! If I could sell that sauce, why, there'd *be* no competition. Nothing on the market could compete."

Connor tossed Beekman a dubious look. "So how did this supersauce get to Arkansas?"

"The town's an Italian settlement. The immigrants came to grow grapes. They found tomatoes grew even better."

"Wonders never cease. Italians in the heart of Dixie. *Arrivederci,* you all."

Beekman ignored the gibe. "It won't be an Italian settlement much longer. It's dying, and I've got the figures to prove it. It'll be dead as a doornail before long. So much then for tradition and family recipes. Ha!"

Connor frowned, took off his sunglasses and glanced at Beekman speculatively. Connor's eyes were the same clear sapphire as the sky behind him, truly remarkable eyes, almost unearthly in their blueness. They'd stared down men as tough as Beekman before.

"You said they still have a festival every year," Connor said. "So they're not giving up yet."

Beekman made a sound of disgust. "The festival's out of hand. It's too big for this...this pack of amateurs. The parking alone is a nightmare. And the lines waiting to eat— a crime. They can't keep it up—the same few people have to do everything. Impossible."

"They have so far."

"But no farther. Their days are numbered. Dee-Lish Foods could take over that festival and streamline it, modernize it, expand it, make it run weeks, not days. Make it serve lunch, as well as supper. Make it twice as big, four times as big, a dozen times as big, the Original Dee-Lish Spaghetti Festival. I could buy out that town and make it my showplace. It could be famous across the country—like Disneyland. Think of it—Beekmanland. Think of the sheer publicity value of the thing."

Connor put his sunglasses back on. "Beekmanland," he said tonelessly. He shook his head.

"Why not?" Beekman demanded. "The day I stop thinking big is the day I'm finished. Vision! That's what a man's got to have—vision."

"But a woman's blocking yours. Too bad."

"She's a stubborn twit," Beekman grumbled. "She even has the nerve to call that two-bit outfit she runs a 'company.'"

"Her own company? No wonder she doesn't need you."

"*She* calls it a company," Beekman said sarcastically. "I call it a joke. Less than two acres to grow spices. One tiny little field. Her 'factory' is a garage, and she does most of the work herself. She sells the stuff at the festival and by mail. Doesn't even advertise. She's a fool—sitting on a gold mine and doesn't know it."

"And I imagine your sweet talk has been well-nigh irresistible," Connor said sarcastically.

"Talk, shmalk. She won't listen. The woman's a bundle of neuroses. She's pining over some dead lover, people say. She hasn't so much as looked at a man in six years. Somehow she thinks she's bound to him and that fool town with spaghetti—it's ludicrous."

Connor cocked his head at a cynical angle. "So what do you want me to do, Morty? Go and offer her more money? You always say everybody has a price."

"Everybody does. It's just a question of finding it."

"What if her price isn't money?"

"What?" Beekman asked, taken aback.

"If her price isn't money? I mean, money's all you talk. What if she speaks a different language?"

Beekman drew back slightly, narrowing his eyes at the blond man beside him. "Then find the language she does speak. And speak it. This time, do better than you did with Fanny Mercator."

Connor said nothing. Once more his smile died and his profile went stony. Fanny Mercator had gone into seclusion after the death of her brother, not her lover, but the parallels between her and the Calvino woman troubled him. Connor could think of no greater waste than living in bondage to the past.

"Well, boy," Beekman challenged, "will you do it? Go to Arkansas and get the recipe?"

For a moment Connor said nothing. Then the corner of his mouth curled in amusement. He shrugged and shook his head. "No. She doesn't want anything to do with you, Morty. She won't deal with me, either."

"So?" Beekman said. "Don't let her know I'm involved at first. Be . . . subtle. Think of it as a game. You're a competitive sort. And, after all, with the yachts at stake, you'd be a fool *not* to think about it, wouldn't you?"

Connor thought about it. In his mind's eye he saw the blue of the Caribbean and on it *The Solitaire,* restored to her old handsomeness. He saw himself on her again, free to roam where he wanted. And on a new adventure, as well, reviving the fleet of yachts into a profitable and exciting business.

All he had to do was go to Arkansas, urge the woman back into the mainstream of life and get Beekman his recipe. It sounded simple, almost playful.

Besides, he had an odd superstitious feeling that this was how Mercator would have wanted it; it was almost as if the old man was sending him a second chance. Perhaps, just perhaps, Connor owed it to Mercator to try to save this woman from herself. Maybe it would make up in some small way for his failure with Fanny Mercator.

THE NEXT DAY Gina came home from her antique shop dispirited. She hadn't made a sale all week, and the festival was almost upon them, robbing her spare time, jumbling her thoughts, crowding her life with extra duties.

Earline had been depressed since her job had ended in May, and she was trying to skimp along on her meager retirement pay. She sewed and costumed elephants until her eyes ached and her fingers stung from needle pricks, hoping to bring more money into the house. She hadn't looked well lately, and Gina was worried about her.

Gina parked her old brown sedan in the drive and crossed the lawn, which needed mowing. She herself had worked last night until after midnight, packaging spices to sell at the festival, and she must do so again tonight.

She adjusted Loren's ring, and its small diamond winked back the afternoon's golden light. Gazing at the stone, she reached deep inside herself and found a smile. She entered the house. From every chair, every shelf, every corner, elephants peered at her with black shoe-button eyes.

"Gina, Gina, Gina!" Earline said, rushing from the kitchen, a spoon in hand. Her white curls were tousled, her apron streaked with flour. She looked like a rotund elf whose baking had just been interrupted.

"What?" Gina asked, her smile growing more natural at the sight of her aunt. "Good news? Calm down."

"Come right in here," Earline said, seizing her by the hand and pulling her into the kitchen. "I've got frosting on the stove, and I can't stop stirring. Oh, Gina, you will not believe this!" Earline made an excited gesture toward the kitchen table. "Sit, sit."

Gina sat, and Earline bustled to the stove. "Earline, what's happened?"

"A magazine's coming," Earline said, stirring harder in her excitement. "A real magazine. Here."

Gina cocked an eyebrow in puzzlement. "You subscribed to a magazine?"

"No, no," Earline said. "A magazine *writer*. Well, really an editor—or is it a publisher? To see about a story on us—on Allegro and the festival! For American Vagabond."

Gina's eyes widened. "The travel magazine?"

"Yes. And he's staying here. Think of it!"

"Here? In Allegro?"

"No," Earline said, "here. In this house. With us. Think of it—right here in this house."

Gina's mouth popped open in surprise. "In our *house?*"

"Yes." Earline nodded, her cheeks flushed. "For a whole week. He'll come this weekend, probably Sunday night."

Gina frowned slightly. "Some stranger's going to walk in here and *camp* for a week?"

Earline tossed her an impatient glance, as if Gina didn't get the point. "It's an honor. And an opportunity. He's going to pay us—he insists."

"Pay?"

"He called from California—Sausalito, I think. He had your name, because of the spices."

"What?"

"Because of the spices. He heard from someone who'd bought your spices at the last festival. He particularly wants to talk to *you*. And see the festival firsthand."

Gina blinked, stunned.

Earline plunged on. "He said he wanted to stay in Allegro, and then he asked where there was here to stay. You know, a motel. And I said, 'Well, there's no motel. But you're welcome to stay here.'"

Gina blinked again, harder.

"And he said—he has such a nice voice, Gina, oh, my! He said, 'Only if I pay you.'"

"Are you sure—?"

"Oh, Gina, listen. He's paying us *seven hundred dollars*. For room and board—he says that's his expense allowance for Allegro, and that's what he'll pay."

With a blank expression, Gina sank back against the chair. "Seven hundred dollars? That's a fortune."

"It is," Earline agreed, beginning to frost the cake. "Think! And don't worry, Gina, I'd do all the work."

"I...I don't mind work," Gina said. "It's just having somebody we don't know—"

"Don't worry," Earline assured her. "I talked ten minutes with him and felt like I'd known him my whole life. He says Allegro could make a *wonderful* story."

Gina's emotions tugged her first one way, then another. National publicity for the festival was wonderful, of course; everyone in Allegro would burst with pride. But still, she hated the idea of a stranger living with them.

Yet seven hundred dollars was a good deal of money. And more important, Earline was happier than Gina had seen her in months.

Gina gave a philosophical shrug. "All right. We'll have a houseguest."

"He really does sound like a *perfect* gentleman," Earline effused. "His name is Munroe. Connor Munroe." With a flourish she made a dramatic swirl on the cake's top, finishing it.

He'd better be a perfect gentleman, Gina thought warily. *If he's not, I'll...I'll drown him in a vat of spaghetti sauce.*

But for Earline's sake, she smiled and said nothing.

CHAPTER THREE

A SULTRY AUGUST SUN beat down as the yellow MG passed the sign that read Allegro—Population 503.

Nothing special, Connor thought sardonically, slowing to obey the speed limit. Just another dusty, dying southwestern town. During his drive across the country, he'd seen dozens just as small, just as sleepy, just as unimpressive. He idly wondered how the woman could be so attached to it.

The town had never been much; he knew that from Beekman's reports. In its heyday, it had been home to slightly more than a thousand people. As in many small towns, its businesses had found it difficult to compete with larger ones in larger towns. One by one they had closed down. Then Allegro's main industry, the tomato cannery, had failed, shut down by the parent company in New York to cut corporate operating costs.

Now, Connor saw, most of the stores around the town's old square were empty, their windows boarded, their sidewalks deserted. Gina Calvino's antique shop, which didn't look to be of much consequence, was among the few still in business.

Allegro's downtown was faded and lifeless. The only thing that distinguished it was a billboard erected next to the town square. The sign was adorned with a picture of the world's most obese tomato. Bright yellow letters shrilled the message: "THE WORLD-FAMOUS ALLEGRO TOMATO FESTIVAL—100 GLORIOUS YEARS!"

Connor shook his head. Nothing struck him as glorious about Allegro. He wanted to settle the business with the Calvino woman, then be on his way, to the Caribbean, he supposed. He had no urge to hang around this one-horse town. None.

He knew her house was just a few blocks from the town square. Turning down a side street, he amused himself by imagining what she looked like.

The detective had snapped a few furtive pictures of her, but they were of poor quality. She was too tall, too thin, had curls that were too unruly, and an incongruous smile that struck him as too wide.

The smile seemed incongruous because she had very little in her life to smile about. She certainly couldn't be smiling inside. The detective had written that "in public she is outwardly cheerful, but popular opinion has it that she still grieves for her dead fiancé."

Connor envisioned her as she must be in private, depressed and lonely, lost in her unvoiced sorrows. Grief had probably dried her up and made her hollow eyed.

He would be gentle when he spoke to her, gradually steering her toward life and sense. He would not let her become another Fanny Mercator. Poor bent Southern flower, he thought. He would prop her up again, whether she liked it or not.

He slowed the car, scanning the houses for the right address. Then he saw it—a large, two-story Victorian house with elaborate fretwork. Although it needed a coat of paint, it was an imposing home, set well back on the lawn.

In the front yard, large weeping willows swayed in the afternoon breeze. Around the porch trellis, a rosebush with pink blossoms twined. Mockingbirds sang from the shade.

Connor pulled into the driveway, parked, and gave the house a knowing squint. It did indeed look as if it harbored a pair of Southern maiden ladies, set in their ways.

Stiffly he got out of the MG; his right foot was aching again. He set his jaw against the pain and began to stride, haltingly, toward the door. He pushed his hand through his wind-tossed hair to comb it off his forehead.

He heard screams and splashes from the far side of the house. Adjusting his sunglasses, he looked with casual curiosity for the source of the noise.

Then, before he knew it, a tall, nearly bare figure charged around the house, squealing in mock fright. As she slammed into him, knocking him backward, something exploded wetly against his chest.

He staggered, but managed to keep his balance, in spite of his throbbing foot. She reeled, but caught herself. They both gasped. Dimly Connor realized that his shirtfront was soaked with water because *she* was soaked—her skin, her curling hair, her faded cutoffs, her bright yellow halter top. She held a flimsy scrap of red in her hand.

"Omigosh," she said, horror filling her brown eyes as her hand closed around the scrap. "My water balloon— I'm sorry. I mean, I'm really, really sorry."

Connor stared at her. He'd spent time on some world-class beaches, yet never had he seen a lovelier expanse of long tanned legs. She was one of those women whose skin the sun kissed lovingly, making it as perfect as fine velvet. Her stomach was flat, her hips slender, and her breasts high and pert under her soaked halter.

Dark curling bangs hung over her forehead, and her eyes were the deepest brown he'd ever seen. Her nose was slim, slightly tilted, and she had a beautiful, generous mouth, the lips slightly parted.

It's the dried-up Southern lady, he thought in surprise, *the one in secret mourning. I'll be damned.*

Her eyes remained fixed on his, horrified. Then she glanced over her bare shoulder as if worried or pursued or both. "War's over," she cried, warning in her tone. "We've got company. War's over. Do you hear me, Wesley?"

There was an ominous beat of silence. Once again her eyes met Connor's.

"No surrender!" screamed a voice from behind an un-trimmed hedge. A blue balloon, filled with water, hurtled through the air. Gina dodged nimbly as it landed with a re-sounding splat in the driveway, flinging water into the air. Both she and Connor blinked as the spray made a brief rainbow in the afternoon sun, showering them.

"Wesley!" Gina threatened. "Stop! I mean it, Wesley Dean—or I reclaim your frog. Truce."

Footsteps pounded around the other side of the house, accompanied by a maniacal youthful cackle. Then an un-easy silence fell, which seemed to signal temporary retreat. Gina took a deep breath and wiped the water droplets from her cheek.

Once more Connor looked her up and down. Her eyes were wide with worry. "Are you all right?" she asked in a voice as slow and rich as molasses.

A smile stirred the corner of Connor's mouth. *Weep no more, my lady,* he thought. *I've come to counsel and console you.*

"Are you all right?" Gina repeated. Her face burned with mortification. Here he was, the editor or publisher or whatever he was—and she had water-ballooned him. His pale blue shirt was drenched, his white slacks, too. Water shone in his hair and spangled his shoes.

He smiled, a slow sideways smile that made her pound-ing heart speed up. He was tall, at least six inches taller than she. Since Gina was five ten and could look most men in the eye, she was disconcerted.

He had thick tawny hair streaked with gold and wore it longer than did most of the men she encountered in Alle-gro. It fell over his forehead at a rakish angle, the blond streaks counterpointing the darker ones.

As he smiled, twin creases appeared in his cheeks beside his natural laugh lines. They were not exactly dimples, but she was hard put not to call them that. For reasons she couldn't fathom, she found this ambiguity fascinating.

Then, just as languidly as he smiled, he raised his hand and took off his sunglasses. Her pulses jumped at the sheer blueness of his eyes. They were as precisely and as electrically blue as the morning glories that climbed the side of the garage. Laugh wrinkles radiated from the outer corners of his eyes, and his brows had a naturally devilish arch.

Oh, my! thought Gina, realizing he was not merely handsome—he was exceptionally handsome. Her hand flew involuntarily to her mouth. It was horrible enough to water-balloon an ordinary mortal; it was somehow worse to water-balloon such a resplendent one.

He smiled more lazily. "Refreshing," he said, his glance flicking up and down her body. "Unexpected—but refreshing."

Close your mouth before a fly walks into it, Gina scolded herself. *You've seen handsome men before. So what?*

"I'm incredibly, unbelievably, inconceivably sorry," she said, stepping up and trying to brush the water from his shirt. Touching him confused her all the more. He had a hard body, surprisingly warm beneath the soaked cotton of his shirt. Embarrassed by the familiarity of her actions, she stepped back immediately.

She was even more embarrassed when he reached out and took her clenched hand. He pried her fingers apart to stare at the ragged scrap of red she still clutched.

"A water balloon?" he asked. He cocked one brow higher, but didn't release her hand. It tingled.

"Wesley Dean...I..." she stammered. "He and I—we—planned this for weeks. I promised to take him to Mott's Pond—to catch a frog. But you get so muddy there...it's the best way to clean up—"

"Whoa," he laughed, his hand tightening more intimately about hers. "Who's Wesley Dean? Whose pond? What frog? Why?"

Gina realized that his fingers were somehow insinuating themselves between hers, linking their hands in an all-too-friendly gesture. Hastily, awkwardly, she drew her hand away and took a step back. She wiped her hand self-consciously on the seat of her cutoffs. He watched the movement with interest, his eyebrow arching more acutely.

She shifted from foot to foot. She was barefoot, of course, which made her feel even more foolish. She folded her arms in front of her with what she hoped was business-like decorum.

She licked her upper lip, and he watched this motion intently as well, his brow quirking slightly higher. "Wesley Dean's our neighbor," she said, nodding toward the house next door.

"A round kid? With glasses? I thought I saw him through the hedge."

"Right." She swallowed and stared down at the drive-way because looking at the man was too distracting. "Wesley Dean and I went to Mott's Pond to catch a frog—"

"Why?"

"For the frog-jumping contest. There's always a frog-jumping contest. At the festival. The festival starts next week."

"The Tomato Festival?" He cocked his head toward the direction of the square. "That the sign advertised? With the tomato as big as a Buick?"

She nodded, her eyes still fixed on the drive. "Yes. Well, the best frogs are in Mott's Pond—"

"Yes. I believe I've heard that."

She glanced at him furtively. His arms, too, were now crossed, and irony gleamed in his incredible eyes.

Quickly she looked away. "Well, you have to wade through the mud and the muck, and so we were going to have a water fight to clean up. Wesley has all these bal-loons—"

"Why? Why does Wesley have 'all these balloons'?"

Gina squared her shoulders and scrutinized the driveway's pavement more fixedly. "Because of the hardware store. When Wesley's father opened the new hardware store—"

"Here?" he asked in disbelief.

Gina shook her head. "Nobody opens anything here. In Milledgeville. But he ordered too many balloons for the grand opening—"

"Wesley's father did?"

"Exactly." She nodded. "So Wesley Dean and I—"

"—had a water-balloon fight to clean Mott's mud off your respective bods," he finished. "And to use up the balloons."

"Exactly."

He laughed. She looked at him again. He didn't seem angry, only amused. But he was drenched, and it was her fault.

"Are you our...guest?" she ventured.

"Yes. What was this? My official baptism?"

She tried to smile but couldn't. She wished he wouldn't regard her so intently; there was something almost like hunger in his look. Yet laughter, too, sparked in his eyes, confusing her.

Gina turned toward his car, resolving to repent for her watery sins. "I'm really sorry. Where's your luggage? I'll carry it in."

His smile faded. "No *woman* carries my luggage."

Ignoring him, she reached into the back seat and drew out a suitcase. "Nonsense," she said briskly, but at that moment Wesley Dean came bursting through the space in the hedge. Behind his glasses, his eyes were wild, and his wet hair stuck up in tufts from his head. His shirt was soaked, so that it clung to his round stomach, and in each hand he held a bulging red water balloon.

"Banzai!" screamed Wesley, thundering across the lawn toward Gina. "No prisoners! Death before dishonor!"

"Run!" Gina cried. She had the suitcase, and with her free hand she seized Connor's elbow and sprinted toward the house, almost dragging him. He hobbled to keep up.

"Wesley Dean, *stop!*" Gina cried. "This is company!"

"He's a spy!" Wesley screamed. "Kill all traitors!"

"What...?" Frowning, Connor glanced over his shoulder. Wesley hurtled after them, his fat legs pumping.

"He's gone into kamikaze mode," Gina panted, pulling him through the front door. She slammed it behind them. "He's overexcited. He gets...that way sometimes." She leaned against the closed door, breathing hard, still clutching Connor's suitcase. She heard Wesley's feet thudding up the porch stairs and a liquid *whump* as a water balloon exploded against the closed door.

Earline bustled from the kitchen, carrying a dish towel. Her white brows drew together. "Gina, have you gotten Wesley Dean into a state again? Who slammed the door? What—?"

The sight of Connor, tall, sun gilded and dripping water onto the hall rug, stopped Earline in midsentence. Slowly she turned her eyes to Gina, who slumped against the door, soaked and cringing.

Her face pained, Earline shut her eyes, as if to block the two of them from her sight. "Mr. Connor Munroe?" she asked between clenched teeth. "From the magazine?"

Gina thought she saw a strange look pass over Connor's face, but it faded so quickly she was certain her mind had played a prank. Maybe he had only been noticing the elephants that seemed to occupy every corner.

"I'm Connor Munroe," he said smoothly. "You must be Ms. Montegna."

"Alas, I must be," Earline said, and opened her eyes. She adjusted a stray white curl and gave Connor a look of frank scrutiny. "I see you've met my niece, Gina—and Wesley Dean."

"Not officially," he said, turning to smile down at Gina. He took her hand again and shook it. "I'm Connor."

"Gina Calvino," she murmured, her gaze falling to the hall rug. Did he hold her hand a second longer than politeness demanded, or was that, too, her imagination?

"Charmed," he said. Impossible as it was, he sounded as if he meant it.

AFTER EARLINE SHOWED Connor to his upstairs room, she almost dragged Gina into the kitchen. None too gently, she began to rub Gina's hair dry with a towel.

"Our guest—from a real magazine," Earline hissed, "and you up and bomb him. I want you to go out of your way to make this up to him, young lady."

"Ouch," Gina protested. "Here. Let me." She took the towel and rubbed her hair. "I'm sorry, but you said he wouldn't be here until tonight. How was I to know?"

"He never said for certain it would be tonight. I'm lucky you didn't hose him down while you were at it. And him— such a nice man. Such a *handsome* man."

Gina hung the towel on a doorknob and nonchalantly ran her hand through her damp curls. "Handsome? I didn't notice." She lied because it seemed unfaithful to Loren to have noticed, so forcibly, how good-looking the man was. Her reaction embarrassed her.

"You're hopeless," Earline muttered between her teeth. "There're fresh clothes in the laundry nook. Go put on something respectable. If you were any wetter you'd turn into a carp. Of *course* he's handsome. What's wrong with you?"

"I don't judge by superficial criteria, such as looks," Gina said rather loftily, rummaging through the dry clothes. Her heart still beat too fast.

"Humph," said Earline.

Gina picked out a fresh pair of cutoffs and her new T-shirt that said *Allegro Tomato Festival—100 Glorious Years!*

Earline immediately took the garments from her and set them back among the stacked laundry. She put her hands on her hips. "Gina," she said sternly, "we're supposed to be making a favorable impression here. Would you mind helping a bit? Wear your blue dress with the stripes. Oh, my stars and garters, you've made me nervous as a long-tailed cat in a room full of rocking chairs."

"Oh, really," Gina huffed, but she complied, picking a half-slip from the laundry basket and taking the dress down from its hanger. She felt guilty at being the source of Earline's jitters and didn't want to worsen things. "Don't be nervous. He seems to think it's funny."

"I'm dying of laughter," Earline practically snapped. "Please be on your best behavior. Really, Gina—water balloons. He'll think we're all loonies."

"I promise," Gina said. "Just calm down, all right?"

Earline shrugged restlessly. "I don't know what to do first—mop this room or the front porch, or offer to clean poor Mr. Munroe's clothes. And, I just remembered, the light bulb is burned out in his closet, *and* I have an elephant to finish...."

Gina shook her head in sympathy and tried to regain her equilibrium. "The first thing is to call Wesley Dean's mother and make sure he's settled down—you don't want any more guerrilla warfare out of him."

"Oh, Wesley Dean!" Earline cried, smacking her forehead in frustration. "He'll lurk like a ghoul out there. Heaven help us all."

She flew off to the living room and started dialing the phone, determined to find a way to calm down Wesley Dean.

Gina shrugged and shook her head. Life was going insane again. It always did when festival approached; she should simply learn to accept it.

A few minutes later, against her will, Gina found herself trundling up the stairs with a new light bulb for Connor

Munroe's closet. She felt stiff and artificial dressed in her best dress and high-heeled sandals for no reason.

She stood as tall as she could and rapped on his door with what she hoped was a dignified air. "Mr. Munroe? I have a light bulb for your closet. Yours is out."

She heard a sound as if he was rising from the bed and fought back a blush. How long had it been since a man had been in this house, had lain on one of its beds? It seemed like an intrusion, almost a sacrilege of some kind.

Connor swung open the door. He had on jeans, a fresh white shirt, still unbuttoned, and he was in his stocking feet. Once more Gina was surprised to have to look up at him— even her high heels didn't make her as tall as he.

The blue of his eyes also surprised her anew, sending an unwanted thrill shivering through her. Eyes that blue should be outlawed, she thought with resentment, and forced herself to remember Loren's soft, serious hazel gaze.

"Ah," said Connor, his disturbing non-dimples appearing. "Let there be light. Come in."

Gina had expected to thrust the light bulb into his hand and make her getaway. Instead she found herself being ushered into his room. Although it was a comfortable room that she had known since childhood, it suddenly felt strange, even dangerous, as if it vibrated with his alien presence.

He leaned one hand against a post of the old walnut four-poster bed and smiled at her. She wished he'd button up his shirt. Too clearly she could see the sculpted planes of his bare chest, bronze against the white of his shirt.

"You're all dressed up," he said, watching her cross the room. "Going out?"

"No." She opened the closet door, stepped inside and tried to unscrew the old light bulb. Stubborn, it refused to budge. Connor watched her struggle with it for perhaps a full minute.

"Let me." Before she could protest, he was at the closet door, leaning inside. When his fingers brushed hers, she snatched her hand away, but couldn't escape the closeness of his body. Her only retreat would be to shrink deeper into the closet, which would be undignified. Instead, she stood like a statue in the semidarkness, trying to ignore his nearness.

His starched shirtsleeve crackled slightly, rustling against hers. She felt the warmth of his tall body and sensed its strength. The scent of his shaving lotion teased her nostrils and reminded her, giddily, of saddle leather and summer breezes.

"Have you and your aunt always lived together?" His voice, so close to her ear, made her backbone prickle.

"As long as I can remember."

His hand on the bulb went still. His shadowy face turned toward hers, and she found she was holding her breath. "Just the two of you here?" he asked.

"And Wesley Dean's frog," she said curtly. "His mother won't let him keep it at their house."

His laugh was soft. Once more she felt an unwanted ripple of awareness dance down her spine.

"Ah. A boy and his frog. Why such interest? Is he a relative, too?" he asked.

"No. He's lonely, and his father's in the hospital. There are no other kids on the block. Besides that, he doesn't exactly—" She stopped, unsure if she should talk so much.

"He doesn't exactly fit in with other kids?" Connor offered, surprising her. She hadn't expected him to be so perceptive. She was relieved to see that the light bulb was, at last, beginning to swivel from its socket.

She nodded mutely, wanting to edge away so that Connor's sleeve wouldn't brush hers, but there was no graceful retreat. His touch made her feel oddly ticklish all over.

He took out the old light bulb and laid it on the closet shelf. He held his hand out to her, and gingerly she gave him the new bulb. He spun it into place. "An only child—Wesley?'' he asked. Somehow he had shifted his position so his body loomed even nearer than before.

"Yes. Yes, he is."

"That can be hard. I know." He gave the bulb a last turn, then tugged on its pull chain. The closet blazed with light, and Gina winced against the sudden brightness.

"Oops," Connor breathed. "Sorry." He gave the chain another tug, letting darkness fall again.

"Well, that works," Gina said briskly and tried to make her way past him, back to light and safety.

"Hold on," he said, a laugh in his voice.

She was alarmed to feel his hands on her upper arms, their warmth burning through the stiff cotton of her sleeves. Her heart hurdled away, leaving her chest empty and panicked. No man had touched her that way since . . . since she didn't want to remember when. What had she and Earline done, letting some California Don Juan have the run of their house?

Before she could protest, he was bending toward her, and she thought she saw a smile on his shadowed face. "Are you really sorry about the water fight?"

Her chest felt more hollow than before. "Sorrier than you'll ever know."

"Prove it."

"What?"

"Prove it. Let me take you to supper tonight. You can explain about Wesley Dean, then show me the town."

Gina's mind raced. His words, his actions had no logic. Why was he holding her so? Why did he ask such a thing? Especially here and especially now. "Mr. Munroe," she said a bit desperately, "we're in a *closet*."

"I'm aware of that."

"It's hardly an appropriate place—"

"I like it. Everywhere else in this house, elephants are watching. Which is something else I wish you'd explain."

He wasn't holding her prisoner, she realized; his touch was so light, so careful, it was actually gentle. She realized she could easily break away from him, yet she didn't. She stayed, her body so close to his she could feel its warmth. He seemed to be teasing her, nothing more, and yet she could not be sure. "Earline makes elephants," she said helplessly.

"I gathered that. Why?"

"For the festival."

"The Tomato Festival?"

"Yes."

"You can tell me about that, too. After all, that's what I came for."

His fingers moved higher, tracing the curve of her upper arms, and she quivered slightly, as if she felt the hand of a ghost.

Her skin chilled as his warm hands closed over her shoulders. She suddenly understood why, from the moment she'd met him, this man disturbed her so.

She realized in dismay that it *was* a ghost that touched her.

It was a long-gone ghost unexpectedly returning, a forbidden and almost forgotten ghost, and its name was desire.

CHAPTER FOUR

GINA WRENCHED AWAY, pushed past him and fled. Connor heard the rapid click of her high heels as she ran down the stairs.

He frowned as he stepped to the bedroom door, then into the hall. Moving to the stair banister, he clasped it and stared down, but she had vanished. The big house seemed to echo around him with silence and emptiness.

For a moment he stood, trying to understand why the silence seemed so absolute, so final. Then he swore under his breath and went back to his room, buttoning his shirt.

He threw himself onto the bed, hands behind his head, and stared at the white ceiling with its old-fashioned light fixture. His fingertips still burned from touching her cool bare arms, her smooth shoulders.

Why, in the name of sanity, did I touch her?

A friendly gesture, he told himself. *A practical gesture, to hold her attention. An ordinary, everyday gesture. That's all. No more.*

No, you fool, you touched her because you couldn't help touching her. It seemed as natural and necessary as breathing. But it wasn't. It was a mistake.

He hadn't been able to keep his hands to himself. And she had flown off as if he'd threatened her very soul.

Connor's frown grew pensive. He hadn't expected her to be beautiful and high-spirited. She was so full of life she made the air around her sing with vitality. How could such a woman be happy loving a man who had been dead for six long years?

"Stop worrying about the woman, you dunce—" he could almost hear Beekman growling in his ear. "Worry about the recipe. It's how you'll get the yachts. It's how you'll get *The Solitaire*."

Connor stared unseeingly at the blank ceiling. In the strangeness of his encounter with Gina Calvino, he had temporarily forgotten why he had come: that she was worth a fleet of yachts.

Not only that, he reminded himself, but Gina, too, was in a position to profit—Beekman was willing to pay her up to sixty thousand dollars. From the looks of the old house and the kind of life she lived, she could use every cent of it.

So for everyone's sake, he needed to be careful and win her trust, not frighten her off. His future, to an extent, depended on it. So did hers, even if she didn't know it.

The first thing to do was to repair the damage he'd done by coming on too strong. His smile faded. How?

The woman lived such a limited, circumscribed life. What could he do to win her over? What would convert her distrust into confidence?

Then the answer came to him, and he smiled again, a bit cynically. The solution was right under the roof. The aunt, of course.

All he had to do was win the aunt over to his side, and Gina would follow. His smile grew more crooked and more certain. He'd court the friendship of the aunt.

It was as simple as that. Then the niece would be his.

GINA HAD ESCAPED to the safety of her bedroom. Her cheeks burned, her face burned, her whole body burned with shame.

She squeezed her eyes shut and breathed deeply until her pulses slowed. Then she opened her eyes again. All around her were reminders of Loren—on every wall, on the bookcases, the dressing table, the bureau top. She looked from one to another, hoping to be calmed by their familiarity.

She crossed to the dressing table, picked up Loren's college graduation portrait and stared at it as if it were an icon.

She remembered the first time he had kissed her. She'd been twelve and he fifteen. Her heart had jumped so unbelievably hard she had truly wondered if she was dying of love.

But how could her heart have leapt almost the same way when Connor Munroe touched her and bent his face toward hers? It was sacrilege.

She bit her lip and set the portrait down. She sat on her bed and hugged the large brown teddy bear Loren had given her for her sixteenth birthday. She squeezed it tightly, as if by doing so she could somehow communicate with Loren.

Why had she felt such a stab of yearning at Connor's touch, such a peculiar thrill at his nearness? She didn't want such feelings. They were supposed to be dead and buried long ago. They frightened her.

And, shamefully, it was a stranger who made them spring back to life. A stranger—a man she barely knew. A man with whom she had nothing in common.

She nuzzled her face against the bear. Why had Connor even touched her in the first place? Had he simply felt slightly lecherous and wanted to see how far the simple-minded country girl would go? She had come to his room all dressed up—maybe he thought she had done so in hope she *might* tempt him. Well, that wouldn't happen again.

She shook her head angrily and set the bear back in place against the pillow. Connor Munroe was tall and handsome—almost too tall and handsome. Such a man must be used to conquests, quick, frequent and easy. She hated having responded to him.

Even more she hated having run away. She must have looked silly, even childish. What would he think? That she was so frightened of men that a mere touch sent her scurrying off, half-hysterical?

She shook her head to clear it, then ran her fingers through her bangs. She shouldn't have run off. She should have said something clever, cold and cutting, then walked away from him, leaving her dignity intact and his in tatters.

Well, it was too late for that, she thought, rising from the bed. Her unexpected surge of response toward him was a mystery, a troubling one. Perhaps it was because his actions had so surprised her. Or because she was still upset over the water-balloon fiasco. Or because this time of year she was particularly vulnerable, thinking of Loren more often than usual.

No matter the reason. It wouldn't happen again. She wouldn't give him the opportunity, and she wouldn't try to look inviting for him. She slipped off the dress, hung it up, kicked off her high-heeled sandals and wriggled out of her panty hose and half-slip.

She rummaged in her bureau for her baggiest pair of cut-offs and stepped into them. Then she went through her closet, searching for her oldest T-shirt. She settled for a faded and oversize red one that said, "Ladies' Sewing Circle and Terrorist Society."

She put on her most ragged running shoes. She took up a tissue and, with a determined gesture, wiped all traces of lipstick from her mouth. Standing before the full-length mirror on her closet door, she inspected herself. The last time she'd worn such an outfit had been to dig worms for fishing.

"If he thinks *this* is dressing for seduction, he's crazy," she muttered. She looked around the room once more, strengthening herself, then stalked into the hall.

"Where are you going dressed like that?" Earline asked when Gina strode through the kitchen. Gina was disconcerted to see Connor Munroe seated at the table, looking right at home. Earline was having coffee with him—and serving him fresh-baked brownies. Gina stuck her nose into the air and acted as if she didn't notice him.

"Gina? Where are you going?" Earline demanded.

"Out," she answered curtly, pushing open the back door. "I'm going to the parish hall to clean the rest rooms."

"That's Snicky Alonzo's job—the janitor's," Earline objected.

"His eyes are bad. He misses things," Gina shot back. "And don't wait supper on me. I'll eat out." She let the door slam behind her.

As she crossed the lawn, she heard Earline's voice behind her, calling from the doorway. "Gina, don't be late. I promised Mr. Munroe you'd show him the town. And that you'd tell him about the spice business."

Gina didn't bother to look over her shoulder. "You do it," she answered as cheerfully as she could. "I've got a busy night—festival, you know."

There, Gina thought with satisfaction. *Let him know I'd rather clean toilets than flirt with him.*

When she got to the parish hall, she found Lindy Marchesi's father, Ralph, had beaten her there; he had already recleaned the rest rooms and had them sparkling.

Yes, he said, it was a shame about Snicky's eyesight, but poor old Snicky needed the job, and Ralph and a few others didn't mind covering for him until Snicky could collect his retirement pay. And Snicky didn't have to know they were helping; he was a proud man—his feelings might be hurt.

Gina smiled. This was why she loved Allegro. Anyone— even a poor old man like Snicky—could count on his neighbors' kindness.

"If you want extra work," Ralph said with a grin, "you might weed the flowers in front of the church. Snicky did it yesterday, but he missed a few. You know."

So it was dusk as she crouched before a bed of marigolds and petunias, pinching off dead flowers and pulling out the clumps of Johnsongrass Snicky had missed. The metallic scent of marigolds mixed with the petunias' sweet one, and a cool evening breeze rose out of the east. A mockingbird sang from the eaves of the church, and Gina was both busy and content. For the moment all thought of Connor Munroe was dispelled.

Then she heard footsteps approaching, slightly halting ones, their sound muted by the grass. Ralph, she thought, snipping back a petunia that had grown too tall. He'd come to say goodbye and ask if she'd taken anything from the toolshed; he would be locking up.

The footsteps stopped beside her, and she looked up with a wide smile for Ralph. The smile died immediately. Not Ralph, but Connor Munroe stood there, towering over her in the deepening twilight. The breeze stirred his thick hair, and streaks of it gleamed muted gold in the sun's fading rays.

"Oh," she said, startled. She sat back on her heels, the long stem of petunia in her hand.

"Hi." His tone was careless, as if nothing had happened between them earlier. "The man at the parish hall..."

"Ralph?" She kept her voice as cool and casual as his.

He nodded. Even in the failing light she could see the smile haunting his lips. "Ralph. He said you'd be here. I thought I'd find you cleaning latrines, not picking posies."

She ducked her head and kept weeding. She could think of nothing to say.

"Your aunt's worried about you," he said. "She's afraid you won't eat."

"I told her—I'd eat out."

"She said you'd probably just grab something at the ice-cream stand up on the highway. She thinks you're too thin. She sent something over for you."

Gina glanced up. He had a white squarish basket hanging from his right hand. She recognized it as Earline's little picnic basket. She clamped her lips together and let her gaze return to the flowers, still saying nothing.

He knelt and held the basket toward her. "Would you mind taking this? I feel like Little Red Riding Hood carrying it around."

Gina cast him another chary look. He *was* smiling, drat him, and she knew why—because he had discomfited her, and he knew it.

He sat down with a sigh, setting the white basket between them. He draped one arm over his knees, then picked up a stem of Johnsongrass and stuck it between his teeth. He looked up at the sky thoughtfully, as if studying the fading colors of the clouds.

"Ah," he said, nodding to himself. "I made the wrong comparison. You don't see me as Red Riding Hood. You probably see me as the wolf. Because of...well, you know."

Gina took a deep breath and pushed a curl out of her eyes. "I have no idea what you're talking about."

"Liar," he said pleasantly.

She shot him an indignant stare.

His smile rose a trifle higher at one corner of his mouth, and even in the failing light she could see his non-dimples play next to his laugh lines.

"What?" she demanded.

"Liar." He said it as a friendly taunt, not an insult. He kept gazing at the clouds. "You know—the closet. I touched you. I shouldn't have. I didn't know you were so...so sensitive. I apologize."

"Don't bother," she said, turning back to her weeding. "Nothing happened. Nothing at all. I got a little claustrophobic, that's all."

"No." His voice sounded suddenly serious. "I'm sorry. Will you accept an apology? It's sincere."

She shrugged. "Of course. Is that all?"

"Why don't you look at me? Did I offend you that much?"

"I can't look at you and weed at the same time."

"It's getting too dark to look at anything. Why don't you quit? We could sit on the church steps. You could eat. Your aunt says you haven't eaten today. That you worked through lunchtime to make time for Wesley Dean."

Gina reached for the basket and set it closer to her. She kept her face as expressionless as concrete. "Thanks. But I can eat alone. I don't need an audience."

"Yes, you do. I promised Earline. Come on. The moon's rising."

So, you're already calling her Earline, are you? Gina thought grimly. *Well, haven't you made yourself right at home, Mr. Munroe.*

"What's the matter?" he said. "Have you knelt in that position so long you're stuck? Do you need me to unbend you and carry you to the stairs?"

"I can unbend myself," she retorted. She stood, then reached down and picked up the basket.

As she straightened again, he rose to stand beside her. For a man so exceptionally tall, his movement was as quick and fluid as a cat's.

"Listen," he said softly, bending so he could look into her eyes, "I came clear from California to see you. I can't afford to have you mad at me. Won't you talk to me? About your family? The festival? The spices? Yourself?"

Gina sighed and rubbed her forearm across her brow. "There's nothing to say about me. If you want to talk about the festival, fine. I'm not interesting. At all."

"Really? Maybe I should get my seven hundred dollars back from Earline and move on."

She went as still as if she were paralyzed. She couldn't let Earline lose all that money because of her. Would he really move on if she weren't more cooperative?

He waved toward the church steps, a movement so leisurely it was almost indolent. "Sit. Eat. Let's get acquainted. I need to know about the festival—that's all."

The crickets clicked in the grass, and a cicada hummed its raspy song. Feeling rebellious yet resigned, Gina carried the basket to the church's cement stairs. She sat as far on one end as she could and set the basket in the middle so that Connor Munroe had to keep his distance.

He didn't seem to notice the unfriendliness of the gesture. Somehow he managed to sit so close that when he bent to open the basket, his wide shoulder brushed her arm.

In spite of the evening's warmth, Gina shivered and drew away. He didn't seem to notice that, either.

"Your aunt worries about you, you know." He reached into the basket and drew out a small plastic bag. "Here— she even sent you a washcloth. You can wipe away any weediness you've acquired."

Gina took it without comment and scrubbed at her hands, which were stained by weeds and sticky with petunia juice.

"Now let's see," Connor mused, rifling through the basket. He seemed so casual, natural and friendly it was hard to distrust him.

"She sent you a thermos of milk—" he handed it to her "—and a ham sandwich. On homemade bread yet. I'll bet the ham's still warm. A great cook, your aunt. There's also some baked beans, coleslaw, and brownies for dessert."

Gina looked askance at the sandwich. It seemed huge, and her stomach was so full of peculiar flutters she had no appetite. "Just give me a brownie," she said. "I'm not hungry."

"You don't want this?" He held the sandwich toward her. "You'll hurt her feelings. I guarantee it's delicious. I watched her make it."

"You eat it. Just give me a brownie."

He handed her two brownies swathed in waxed paper and unwrapped the sandwich. "It's your loss," he said with a shrug. He bit into the sandwich. "Mmm. The woman's a genius. And those brownies—wow. Is your spaghetti really as good?"

She took a nibble of her brownie. She knew Earline made wonderful brownies, but to Gina this one was as tasteless as sawdust. All she was conscious of was the uncomfortable nearness of Connor Munroe. That, and the strange conflict that while her emotions said to trust him, her mind argued she must not. *Be careful,* she thought. *Be cool.*

"It's not my spaghetti," she said. "Just the spices in the sauce. It's my great-great-grandmother's combination. I had nothing to do with it."

He cocked a skeptical eyebrow. "You keep the secret, don't you?"

"Yes."

"Why's it so secret?"

Gina finished the brownie and pushed the other toward Connor. She spanked her hands clean, then locked them around her knees. She stared at the rising moon. "It's secret because it's always been secret. It's a family tradition."

"I see. Want some beans? Coleslaw?"

"No. And I doubt very much if you *see.*"

He sighed and picked up the fork Earline had packed. "I wouldn't eat all this, except to keep Earline's feelings from being hurt. A lovely woman, Earline. You say I don't see. All right. Make me see."

She kept staring at the moon. "That recipe—it was all my great-great-grandmother had from the old country. It was—" Gina struggled to verbalize the importance of the recipe "—her only wealth. Her only independence. Times were hard. If she wanted something a little extra, well, she could get it by selling spices."

She sensed Connor watching her, and her mouth suddenly felt dry. She licked her lips. "She had four sons and one daughter. She wanted to leave her daughter something—something that would make life a little easier. It was the recipe. And my great-grandmother left it to my father, and my father left it to me."

Connor leaned back lazily against the stairs. He stretched out his long legs and began to eat the last brownie. "And?" he said, challenging her to go on.

Stars began to wink into sight. She studied them, instead of looking at him. "And," she said, her tone cool, "we've always been happy to share it for the festival. It's like a gift that only we can give the town. We used to own land, but now there's only the spice field left—it's our heritage. And besides that, whenever we needed some little thing, well, there was the spice money."

"How? Give me a concrete example."

She watched the stars and smiled to herself. "Christmas presents," she murmured. "Grandma always used it for Christmas presents. And when she and Grandpa celebrated their fortieth wedding anniversary, she paid for a trip to Hot Springs for both of them. We never knew how long she had to save for it—maybe all forty years."

"And your father?" His voice was serious.

Gina's dreamy expression faded. "My mother was sick when I was small. That's why Earline came to live with us. There were bills. My father worked his way up to foreman at the tomato cannery—but then it closed. The spice money helped us get along until he found another job. He had to work in Milledgeville. There weren't many jobs left here."

"And you?" His voice was lower and even more serious than before. It was a haunting voice, Gina thought distractedly, a husky baritone with an accent she couldn't pinpoint. Sometimes it gave her strange interior tickles. She felt them now.

She tried to shrug them away and looked at the ground instead of the stars. The vastness of the sky had made her slightly dizzy.

"Me? Well, it helped me set up the antique shop. It helps in emergencies. Like when the television broke last year. Earline couldn't live without her programs."

He made no reply. They sat in silence, listening to the crickets and the rasp of the cicada. Connor seemed to be trying to be companionable, nothing more. Somewhere a whippoorwill sounded its lonely cry.

The black shape of a bat skittered across the full moon. The bat was followed by another. It, too, was momentarily outlined against the moon. Gina couldn't help it. She laughed.

One of Connor's brows drew down, and he gave her a dubious smile. "What's so funny? The bats?"

She nodded. "Father Haney and Snicky tried everything to get rid of them. I was afraid this summer they'd succeeded. But they haven't. We still have 'em—bats in our belfry."

"What?" He gave a short laugh of disbelief.

She nodded again, smiling. "We do. They live in the church steeple. Here in Allegro, we really do have bats in our belfry. Crazy, isn't it? I love it."

She realized he was studying her with that combination of intensity and mockery that had, right from the beginning, so disturbed her. The blue of his eyes glinted almost silvery in the moonlight and a muscle in his cheek gave a minute twitch. Her eyes suddenly seemed locked with his, and her smile fell away again. Her heart kicked against her chest.

"You've got a nice smile," he said tonelessly, almost clinically.

Gina forced herself to look away. She scanned the sky for signs of the bats, but all she could see were the dazzling stars.

"Your aunt—your great-aunt," he amended, "really does worry about you. She wants you to be happy."

"I am happy," Gina said to no star in particular.

"She told me about him. About your fiancé. Why you wear the ring." He paused. "I'm sorry."

She stiffened, unable to say anything. She managed to take a deep breath, but it hurt. "I don't want to talk about it," she said from between her teeth.

"To me? Or to anybody?" he asked in the low voice that made her uneasy.

"To anybody. There's nothing to talk about. It was a long time ago."

She ducked her head and tried to busy herself packing the picnic leftovers into the white basket. He started to help her, and his hand accidentally closed over hers as they both reached for the fork. Her flesh was cold to the touch, his hot.

She sucked in her breath with dismay and jerked her hand away as if she'd been stung.

He stared at her, his face almost rigid in the moonlight. He'd drawn his hand back, too. "I didn't mean anything by that." His voice was taut. "It was an accident."

Suddenly Gina's emotions, tumultuous ever since Connor had first appeared, threatened to overwhelm her. She felt foolish and weak to have snatched her hand away so desperately, and she had an irrational urge to cry. Hastily she blinked, forcing the tears back.

"Is this where it would have happened?" he asked, tilting his head to indicate the church. "Where you would have married him?"

She blinked, nodded, and blinked again. "Yes."

He gave a ragged sigh. "So maybe we should go someplace else. Would that be better?"

"I should go home," she said, not answering his question. "I have work to do."

She reached for the basket at the same moment he did, and they both stopped, as if frozen, their hands poised above its handle.

"Go ahead, Gina," he said in his huskiest voice. "I won't touch you. I promise. Just talk to me. You said you would."

Once more he drew his hand back and watched as her fingers closed around the basket handle. "Another time," she said, not looking at him. "I really can't talk tonight—I have too much to do."

"What? Label all those packages of spices? Earline's doing it. So you can talk to me. And so you can rest a little. She also worries that you work too hard. Make her happy, all right? Just talk to me, that's all."

"Earline shouldn't be doing my job," Gina said, frustrated. "She has an elephant to finish."

"She wanted to," Connor insisted. "She's concerned about earning her keep, you know. Since she lost her job at the school."

"Oh, good grief," Gina muttered, shaking her head. "Earline—*earn her keep?* She's the dearest person in the world. But what's she done? Told you our whole life story?"

When she rose, he did, too, and stood looking down into her eyes. This time she didn't look away. "I love Earline," she said. "But she shouldn't tell you about our...our private lives."

"She was being friendly, that's all. I consider her a friend."

"Friend?" Gina challenged. "You hardly know her. You can't be friends just like that." She snapped her fingers almost in his face.

"Gina," he said, his voice dangerously low, "people fall in love just like that." He snapped his fingers back at her. "If you have love at first sight, why can't you have *like* at first sight?"

"Because nothing genuine happens that fast," she said, starting down the walk. "Things like...like friendship take time. If they're real. If they're going to last."

"Where are you going?" He kept his place on the bottom step, staring after her. The moonlight gleamed on his hair.

"Home. I'm walking home."

"No. I'll drive you. My car's just over there." He nodded toward the parish hall.

"I'd rather walk, thanks," she said, and struck off in the direction of home.

"Gina!" His call was so edged, so urgent that she paused and looked back.

He stood outlined against the church, both man and building bathed in the platinum of moonglow. "Wait. We have more to talk about. For instance, I know Morton Beekman. You share your information, and I'll share mine. Interested?" he challenged.

Beekman, Gina thought, feeling almost dazed. *He knows Beekman? How? What's he got to do with this?*

The old man's name was like a magic spell that kept her rooted to the sidewalk. Helplessly she watched as Connor left the stairs and walked toward her. He seemed to enjoy her bewilderment.

"Don't worry, Gina," he said when he reached her side. "I said I wouldn't touch you, and I won't. You're as safe with me as if you were wearing a chastity belt and had swallowed the key. Which, I suppose, in a way you have."

His lips curved slightly, but there was no mirth in his smile. It was bitter, and it was hard, and it was mocking.

Whether it was her he mocked or himself, she could not tell.

CHAPTER FIVE

GINA WAS SO MUCH HARDER to handle than Connor had anticipated that he was both frustrated and intrigued. The combination had made him reckless. He shouldn't have mentioned Beekman—but he had. Now his conversation would have to slither around the subject.

"Beekman?" she demanded, her stance defiant. "What do you know about him?"

Connor smiled his most innocent smile. "I told you—I'll trade with you. Tell me about the town, the festival and yourself. Then I'll tell you the little I know about Beekman."

"How do you know him? If you're a friend of his, you're no friend of mine."

"There's no love lost between Beekman and me. Anybody in business in California tangles with him sooner or later. I heard he's after your recipe. Everybody between San Francisco and Monterey knows it. That's how I got interested in the festival—and you. That's all."

Even in the falling darkness, he could see the glitter of dislike in her beautiful eyes. "You don't stop at anything, do you?" she asked bitterly. "First you threaten me over Earline's money, now you drag Beekman into it."

He smiled again but wondered how long he could keep it up. He hadn't liked bringing up the money and didn't intend to do it again. He didn't like bringing up Beekman, either. But he wanted her attention, dammit, and he intended to have it.

How long he could pretend nonchalance was another matter. She wasn't what he'd expected, and she stirred unexpected and foreign emotions in him. But he had to appear calm. He kept on smiling, and he argued as glibly as he'd ever argued in his life.

He admitted he had a few tidbits of information about Beekman—that was all. But he was used to asking questions, not answering them. He was a gatherer of news, not a dispenser; that wasn't his line.

Fair was fair, he said. She must come with him, give him more background information, just as Earline had asked. Only then would he talk of Beekman.

On he argued, until she finally gave a grudging nod and agreed to go with him. By that time he was disgusted with both himself and her. With himself, because he was reduced to such chicanery, and with her for wasting her spirited loveliness on a dead man and a dying town.

Would she ever let go of her ghostly lover? Would her thoughts always circle, leading back to a man in his grave? What should he say to such a woman? What could he say?

He wondered how long he could keep up his smiling facade. *Charm her,* he thought. But Gina Calvino seemed impervious to his charm. He set his jaw and vowed to be patient. But still the recklessness churned, deep within him, filling him with discontent.

HOW'D HE EVER TALK ME into this? Gina wondered. She'd found herself settling primly into the MG's passenger seat as Connor walked to the driver's side.

Hesitantly she touched the leather upholstery, as if proving to herself it was real. She was reminded of Loren, who had dreamed of owning a sports car. Throughout their courtship, he'd driven a dented white pickup truck.

She tried to imagine Loren in this car, its top down, the moonlight silvering his features. But she couldn't, and her inability to picture him somehow saddened her and made her angry at herself.

"Show me Allegro in the moonlight," Connor said as he settled behind the wheel. It was *his* features that the moonlight silvered, *his* strong hand that locked with such casual sureness on the steering wheel.

Gina looked away from him, propping her elbow on the car door, her chin in her hand. She stared moodily at the empty drive. No other car was in sight. The church was on a hill, and below it spread the lights of the town.

"That's Allegro," she said flatly. She nodded up toward the sky. "That's the moonlight."

"You're supposed to give me a tour of this town. What wonders will I see?"

"None. A tour'll take all of ten minutes. Then you can tell me your 'tidbits' about Beekman and take me home."

He nodded calmly, then put the car into gear and backed out of the church parking lot. Ralph's car was gone, and the parish hall was dark. The only nearby lights were within the church, so that the stained-glass windows shone softly in the night, like multicolored jewels.

"It's a nice little church," Connor said. "Looks old. Is it?"

"Yes."

The car moved silently and swiftly through the darkness, and the wind tousled Gina's hair. It occurred to her that she had never ridden in a convertible before.

"How old?" Connor asked, teasing. "Could you part with that much information, at least? Or would it break your jaw?"

"Ninety-eight years old," Gina said. "That's why the town had the first two festivals. To build it. Part of the money still goes to it. That's why it's exceptional."

"Right. The famous festival. What else does it pay for? Not the nightlife around here, because there isn't any."

The car smoothly took a curve that headed south toward the country darkness, rather than west, back into the heart of Allegro.

"You took the wrong turn," Gina said, looking at him warily. "Town's back that way."

Connor kept driving into the velvety dark, away from the lights. "There's another building up here I'm curious about. It looks deserted."

"The tomato cannery?" Gina said, looking at him in disbelief. "You want to see an empty tomato cannery? At night? It's been closed for years."

"It was the heart of this town's industry, wasn't it?"

Gina leaned her chin on her fist again and stared at the moon-washed fields. She disliked seeing the factory as it was now, so silent, so deserted. She remembered when it worked overtime during the harvest season, and how, when the wind was right, she could stand on the front porch of the house and smell its tangy scents on the summer breeze.

Once its graveled parking lot had been full of workers' cars, but now the lot was going to grass and weeds and scrub.

In summers, she used to bring her father his lunch here, packed in Earline's white picnic basket. They would sit in the shady grove in the meadow behind the cannery. There was a pond in the meadow, and as they ate, they would watch the egrets and red-winged blackbirds visiting the water.

Connor spoke again, startling her out of her reverie. "I said," he repeated, "it was the heart of the town's industry once, wasn't it?"

"Yes. Once." She didn't look at him. As they rounded a curve, the building appeared, surrounded by weeds, its roof starting to sag. She regarded it sadly.

When she was a child and saw the building on a night such as this, its metal sides had sparkled. She'd thought of it as a magical place, full of technical marvels, shining like a wizard's workshop in the moonlight. Now she saw it for what it was: an old building rusting from disuse, not a jot of magic to it.

Connor pulled onto its overgrown drive and parked. He gestured toward the building. "Tell me about it. What it meant to the town. What it means now that it's closed."

Gina didn't like his bantering tone, for she sensed scorn in it. "Once it meant jobs. Now it means no jobs. Wood mice, possums and spiders live in it. And memories, I suppose. A lot of memories should be drifting around."

"Memories." He stretched his arm along the back of the seat. Gina tensed, but he did not so much as brush her shoulder. "So tell me some memories."

She took a deep breath, grateful he'd kept his word and not touched her. Yet a strange discontent whispered along her nerve ends, something almost like regret. "Just memories." She shrugged, but it was as if he had summoned the memories and now, relentless, they surged back, refusing to be denied.

She gestured toward the meadow, where the elm and maples stood. "Summers, Earline would pack a picnic lunch, and I'd ride my bike here, and my father and I would eat in that grove. He always had stories. It was like every person in the cannery was a character in a novel that went on and on."

He shook his head and gave her a sideways glance. "A cannery like a novel. Has anybody bought the movie rights?"

"Go ahead and laugh," she said with spirit. "There *were* stories here. Sad ones and glad ones and funny ones."

He threw his head back and stared at the star-strewn sky. "My God, look at the stars," he said softly. "I saw stars like this once in Australia. In the outback. Amazing."

He paused and kept staring at them, not looking at her. "So tell me some cannery stories," he said at last. "One of each kind. A sad one, a glad one and a funny one."

She, too, looked up at the stars, so many that the sky seemed awash in clouds of them. For some reason, she wanted to make Connor understand how special Allegro was, but she didn't know if she had the skill to put it into words. Or, if she could, if Connor was the kind of man capable of understanding.

"One summer," she said softly, "one of the workers died. His name was Ken Marchesi. The day he was buried, people noticed a dog at the cemetery, right at the grave. And somebody said, 'That's Ken's dog.' People tried to take it away, adopt it, but it would never eat, and it always escaped and went back. Always."

"Oh, no," Connor said, shaking his head. "Don't do this to me. Not a faithful-dog story. I'm too jaded."

"You asked," she answered, piqued by his cynicism, "so listen. Yes, it's a faithful-dog story. And yes, it did stay by the grave. The cemetery's right down the road from here—about half a mile. Every single day at noon, somebody came from this cannery to feed that dog, because it wouldn't leave Ken's grave. Every single day."

She looked at him and he was still staring at the stars, a crooked smile, half-derisive, at the corner of his mouth.

"Oh, go ahead and smirk," Gina said contemptuously. "I'm telling you that every day for seven and a half years, someone came from here to feed that dog. My father himself did it on Sundays. And he and Snicky Alonzo built it a little shelter, so it wouldn't freeze in the winter or get rained on in the rain."

Connor kept his mocking smile. "And when it died, everyone contributed to a monument of the finest marble—'Here Lies Man's Best Friend—Loyal to the End.' Children and old ladies come from miles around to admire it and weep."

Gina narrowed her eyes at him. "No," she contradicted. "Snicky found the dog dead on the grave one Friday in December. So he came and told my father that they should

probably bury the dog at Ken's feet. But he didn't know
what to do, because the church would never allow it.''

"And?" Connor cocked an eyebrow.

"He was right. Father Haney couldn't let them bury it—
the cemetery's, you know, sacred ground. So my father said,
'Well, we won't put him in a position where he has to say
no.' They waited until night and they buried the dog at Ken's
feet.''

Gina got a lump in her throat remembering. "Snicky
asked my father if they were committing some kind of sin,
burying the dog in the graveyard like that. And my father
said, 'Snicky, God has to judge that, not me. He'll let us
know when we get to the other side.''

She swallowed hard, then smiled at what her father had
done. "The ground was frozen so hard it took nearly an
hour to dig a grave. And my father wrapped the dog in one
of his old jackets. They covered the grave and patted snow
back over it. But they made sure Ken and that dog would
stay together. *That's* the kind of town this is.''

He turned to face her, his eyes glinting in the moonlight.
"No," he said and shook his head.

"What do you mean, no?" she asked, taken aback. Did
he think she was lying?

"No," he repeated. "I don't think that's the kind of town
this is. I think that's the kind of man your father was.
There's a difference.''

She shook her head adamantly. "This town helped create my father, and my father helped create this town. There's
no difference. None.''

"And you've got tears in your eyes because some damn
dog is pushing up daisies down the road.''

"I do not have tears in my eyes," Gina said between her
teeth, and until that moment, she hadn't realized that she
had. And she wondered why his mood should have shifted
toward something like anger or resentment.

"Well, I'd be happy to wipe them away," Connor said, frowning harder. "But then I'd have to touch you." He reached into his back pocket and fumbled until he found a handkerchief. He thrust it at her. "Here. Wipe your eyes. Blow your nose. Do what you've got to do. And never let me ask you for another sad story. I can take them just fine, but you're a pushover."

"I am not," Gina said, but she still had to dab at her eyes with his handkerchief.

"So tell me a glad story," he said in disgust. "Cheer up, will you? Jeez, I hate it when women cry. I mean, I really hate it."

Gina gave a final frustrated sniff into the handkerchief and then crumpled it in her lap. She raised her chin. "A glad story," she said, setting her jaw. "All right. There was another worker—Gary Orsini. For years he and his wife wanted a baby. But they just couldn't. Then finally she got pregnant, but it was a very difficult delivery. Gary was with her, the whole time, about eighteen hours. But it was a beautiful baby—a little girl—and she was perfect."

Gina stared at the old building and smiled, shaking her head. "He came back to work the next day, and the people at the cannery had tied the biggest pink ribbon you ever saw around the whole *building*. With a bow and everything. The women in town had made it out of old bed sheets—stayed up the night before dyeing them pink, and cutting them, and sewing them into this great big ribbon. And they made a big banner out of pink, too, that read It's a Girl. People said, when he saw it his face lit brighter than anything you ever saw."

She laughed. "It must have been the biggest ribbon in the world. There were pictures of it in papers as far away as Little Rock. We've still got it, folded up in a big box at the museum. Nobody knows what to do with it, but nobody can bear to throw it away."

Connor sighed, his mouth taking a downward ironic quirk. "Do you know the look you get on your face when you talk about this town? You look like you're in love or something."

"I *am* in love with it. I always have been. I always will be."

"A place is just a place." He shook his head, frowning.

"Not if it's your home. Don't you have any feelings for your home?"

His expression grew harder. "No."

"Where is your home, anyway? California?"

"No. Nowhere. Anywhere."

"Well, you had to grow up someplace," Gina said, perplexed.

"No. A lot of places." He turned to face her. "Look, we're not here to talk about me. We're talking about Allegro. You said there were funny stories about this place." He nodded at the abandoned cannery. "Tell me one."

Gina made an impatient gesture. "And you were supposed to tell me about Morton Beekman. It's time you did. It's the only reason I came with you."

His face was still stolid, almost stony. "One more story. Then we trade. You go first."

She smoothed her hair again, brushing the curls back from her forehead. "A funny story," she said, musing. "There were dozens. Hundreds. It's hard to choose. Once, a hoot owl found a way in and out of the cannery. It was building a nest in the attic. Snicky Alonzo tried to catch it—"

"Snicky Alonzo is beginning to assume mythic proportions in my mind," Connor said out of the side of his mouth.

"Snicky *did* catch it," Gina said, ignoring the gibe, "but he was trying to take it outside, and it got loose. It got frightened and flew into a wall and fell smack into this enormous vat of catsup."

"An owl in the catsup," Connor said tonelessly.

"Which was not a laughing matter," Gina said, shaking her head, "because the owl sank, and it was going to drown. Nobody could see it to fish it out, so somebody was going to have to get into the vat and feel around for it. There was a young man named Curtis Bates. He never talked. He was famous for being closemouthed. But he dived right into the catsup and pulled the owl out, which was very brave, because the catsup was hot.

"Well, they got Curtis out, and he was fine, and so was the owl, once they cleaned it up. But my father'd been outside the whole time and didn't know anything had happened. He saw Curtis walking out of the cannery, all covered with catsup and heading for the pond. My father couldn't believe his eyes. So he said to Curtis, 'Curtis, what on earth have you been doing?'

"Curtis thought a moment, then said, 'Owl diving.' Then he just walked on, like nothing had happened.

"Well, the story about the owl spread really fast, and when my father came home, he said to us, 'You'll never guess what happened today. Most amazing thing I ever heard of—truly amazing.' Earline said, 'You mean the owl falling into the catsup?' My father laughed. 'No,' he said, 'more amazing than that. Curtis Bates said two words in a row.'"

She smiled broadly at the memory of her father's humor, but Connor, watching her, didn't laugh.

Gina's smile fell away, and she suddenly felt foolish, like someone who has just told a joke that fell flat. "Well, I guess you had to know Curtis. Otherwise it's just a kind of silly story. I'm...sorry."

"No," he said softly, his gaze on her lips, "it was a good story. I liked it. I liked the way you smiled."

She looked away, embarrassed.

"What happened to them all?" he asked. "I know Snicky works at the church. And your father's...gone. What happened to the other people? Gary Orsini and his wife and baby? Curtis Bates? Did he ever say anything longer than 'owl diving'?''

"I don't know," Gina whispered, staring at the empty building. "They're all gone now. Curtis moved to Oklahoma to work on his cousin's farm. Gary and Kathy and the baby left. He got a job in Hot Springs. I miss them. And the baby's not a baby anymore. She's a big girl now—eight years old. I wish I could have watched her grow up.''

"Please. Don't go wistful on me again," he said gruffly.

She turned back to face him. He wore an expression of rigid control, the muscles in his jaw tense. His eyes flicked over her face, and there was something so intense in his glance that her heart jumped. She tried to keep her own expression neutral and aloof.

"Tell me about Morton Beekman," she said.

"I could think of a million things I'd rather talk to you about than Morton Beekman. I don't like him much.''

"That makes two of us.''

"You won't like what he has to say about your precious town, either.''

Gina's hand tightened around the handkerchief. "Oh. That.''

"Yes. That. He's the one who told me about this place. I wouldn't have known if it wasn't for him.''

She lifted one shoulder scornfully. "He thinks Allegro is . . . is doomed or something. Well, we're alive and kicking, thank you.''

"Gina." He said her name carefully, almost thoughtfully, and he was frowning slightly.

His tone, the seriousness of his expression startled her. "What?"

He glanced restlessly up at the stars, then back at her, frowning harder. "He's right.''

Something deep inside her seemed to clench and grow cold. She stared at him in dismay.

"I've seen his reports," Connor said with a gesture of disgust. "I've seen all his damned data. The projections. And he's right. This town can't last forever. It can't even last another twenty-five years. Probably not another ten."

"That's not true," she said.

"A town's like a person." His voice was harsh. "It's born. It grows. But it can get feeble. And die."

"No," she said stubbornly, hating the comparison.

"Yes. And this town's already at the feeble stage. This cannery's been closed six years. Nobody's going to reopen it. The mother company can't unload it. It's a dead property. You've got no industry here. And none coming in."

"We're more than industry. We're people."

"Look at your town square. It's half-dead. I saw the stores this afternoon—all boarded up. The hardware store, the variety store, the movie theater, the clothing store. Even the grocery store, for God's sake. All you've got are a couple of little convenience shops up on the highway."

"There's nothing sinful about a convenience store," Gina argued. "That's no sign of anything."

"Will you get that stubborn look off your face and listen to me? This town can't support anything bigger than a convenience store anymore. You want to shop at a supermarket, you drive six miles to Milledgeville—where the real business action is. You want clothes? The same. You want anything of consequence at all? It's in Milledgeville."

"Milledgeville, Milledgeville—you sound like a broken record."

"*You* sound like the broken record. All you say is, 'No, no, it isn't happening.' But it is. There are six miles between here and Milledgeville. Farmland. And how long can those farmers hold out, Gina? Not long, and you know it."

"No," she said. "No."

"Yes," he said, leaning closer to her. "One by one they'll realize they're going to be better off selling that land. Milledgeville's growing fast. Developers will snap it up. It'll happen. If Allegro survives at all, it'll only be as a suburb of Milledgeville. And it'll be lucky to do that."

"No!" She tried to inch away from him, but he had her cornered. He bent closer still.

"This cannery's closed, your grade school closed this year. How long since the high school shut down? Ten years? How long since you've had a doctor in this town? A dentist? Fifteen years? Your cute little festival keeps the volunteer fire department supported, but is it really worth it?"

"What do you care about it all?" she demanded, trying to push him away. But his chest was as inflexible and immovable as a wall. Its heat and hardness made her hand feel as if it were burning, and she snatched it back.

"Why do I care? I care about it for your sake, believe it or not," he said, the muscles in his jaw tightening.

"My sake?" she said in disbelief. She realized she was breathing hard and so was he.

"Your sake. I told you I know Morton Beekman. He usually gets what he wants. You're smart to hold out for more money, but you'd be stupid to hold out forever. I know how much money you make a year—with your antiques and your spice business. It's pretty pathetic. I know how much Earline's making in retirement pay, and it's not much, either."

"How—"

"I even know how much money she makes selling those crazy elephants. I know how much money—to the penny— you have in your checking account and how much in savings. You don't believe me? All right. Savings account—a hundred and twelve dollars and eighteen cents. *That's* your life's savings, Gina."

"How do you know—?"

"You and Earline live in a house too big and too old for you. It's in disrepair and getting worse. You need storm windows. You need a new water heater. You need a new furnace. You need a new roof, for God's sake."

She could not help herself. She struck him on the shoulder with her fist, as hard as she could. "Stop it!" she cried. "Just stop! How do you know all this, anyway? It's a violation of my privacy." For emphasis, she hit his shoulder again.

If she'd hurt him, he didn't show it. The set of his face showed no emotion at all except cold determination. "I know it because Beekman knows it. He's had a detective check you out."

"A detective?" The tide of rage that swept over her made her feel faint. "A detective?"

"Yes. From Milledgeville. I've seen the files on Allegro, Gina. And the files on you. And I've seen enough of this town to know Beekman's pretty well right about everything. I'm sorry it's true, but it's true."

Gina glared at him. "*He* sent you, didn't he?" she said with a cold and sudden flash of insight. "You don't have anything at all to do with a magazine. You lied to us and tricked us. You came for *him.*"

His expression was of distaste. He hadn't meant to tell her as much as he had. It was another tactical error, a bad one. He was tempted to lie to her, but found he hadn't the stomach for lying. He was sick of it. He was sick of having let Beekman tempt him into the whole damned mess.

"I do have something to do with a magazine. But you're right. He sent me. To talk you out of the recipe."

She stared at him, her mouth slightly open in shock. He was not in the least surprised when she drew back her hand and slapped it across his face so hard he felt his teeth rattle. He took it without protest because he knew he deserved it.

His silence, his lack of response, seemed only to infuriate her more. So he was not surprised when she set her teeth together and slapped him a second time, even harder than the first. He was not even surprised that it hurt as much as it did. For so slender a woman, she packed a lot of power, though he supposed it was fed mostly by anger.

What surprised him was that when she drew back her hand to slap him a third time, he seized her by the wrist and stopped her. "No," he said, gripping her wrist tightly. "No. Not that again. This."

And he bent and kissed her until his heart seemed ready to hammer through his chest, and all the fiery stars above Allegro seemed to be spinning in his head.

CHAPTER SIX

CONNOR'S LIPS DESCENDED on her own with such passion-
ate certainty that Gina was stunned. *This is not happening.
This can not be happening,* she thought. His mouth, warm,
hungering and expert, seemed some kind of startling sen-
sual hallucination.

Turbulent emotions flooded her consciousness like a tide
of shadows, until she drowned in their depths. All rational
thought swept off into darkness.

Then, magically, confusion ceased. The world resolved
itself into the simplicity of pure sensation. Gladly she let it
take her.

Her senses swam with awareness of his lips as they at once
stole pleasure and bestowed it. How burning, how foreign,
how intense and ardent was his touch, and how easy it was
to lose herself in it.

Gina knew his kiss expressed anger, but it expressed far
stronger and more complicated feelings, as well. Anger was
mixed into her own response, too, for she held her lips up to
his almost in defiance. It was as if both she and Connor had
boiled past the point where words could communicate. Only
touch was powerful enough to express the maddening cur-
rents that pulsed between them.

The arm that coiled so tightly about her waist was both
wanted and unwanted. The harsh pressure of his chest
against her breasts felt wrong, yet breathtakingly right. She
yearned for the mouth that spoke to hers with such silent
eloquence, but resented it, as well.

Oh, Gina thought, her lips parting beneath his, it was wonderful to be held, to be kissed, to be desired and to desire again. Years had passed since she had kissed so—perhaps never before had she been kissed so. For a happy second she had the sensation of someone who has long been wandering lost and alone and who has finally come home.

A blissful yearning sighed through her, and she lifted her free hand to touch Connor's cheekbone, to explore the curve of his jaw, stroke the thickness of his hair. She gave herself up to him with an eager longing so forceful it was almost like sorrow.

His hand released her wrist and rose to tangle in the silky spill of her hair and to draw her, breathless, more deeply into his kisses. Freed, her hand fell, trembling, to rest upon his shoulder. Her fingertips felt the warm live play of his muscles beneath the crisp cloth of his shirt.

His shoulder was wide and thick with sinews, unlike Loren's, which had been lean and wiry. His kisses were restive and hot, whereas Loren's had been tender, restrained, almost sedate....

Loren. A chill welled up her spine, pinching at her brain. A cold suffocation seized her lungs, shooting pain through her chest.

Loren, she thought, stricken. He was truly, literally, the only man she'd ever kissed, ever held, ever wanted—until now. Until this terrible and disgraceful moment.

She wrenched her head sideways to free her lips from the touch of Connor's. At the same moment she spread both hands against his chest, pushing him away with all her might.

To her surprise he drew back immediately, his breathing ragged. He no longer touched her, but she still seemed to feel the beat of his heart against hers, a phantom, ghostly drumming.

Keeping her face turned from his, she opened her eyes. There, in the darkness, stood the abandoned cannery, backed by the starry sky. The decaying building no longer seemed like a wizard's workshop to her. She knew it never would seem so again.

And she no longer seemed like Loren's faithful love. She felt stupid and cheap. She'd been disloyal to Loren, she'd been disloyal to herself, she'd been disloyal to the idea of love itself.

What was she, a hypocritical, sex-starved spinster? Ready to fling herself into any arms, even those of a man who was a liar, a trickster and an enemy?

"Take me home." Weariness shook her voice. "Take me home, then get your things out of our house and go."

She stared at the cannery. It blurred through her unshed tears.

Connor's voice was tight. "I promised I wouldn't touch you. I'm sorry. I hadn't counted on— Oh, hell." She heard him hit something, maybe the dashboard, with the flat of his hand.

She straightened, squared her shoulders and faced him. "So? It wasn't the first lie you told. You tell so many lies you probably can't keep track."

He looked her up and down. A slow, bitter smile tugged the corner of his mouth. "At least I don't lie to myself."

She wiped the back of her hand across her mouth, as if to scrub away the memory of his kiss. It was an empty gesture. Her mouth still tingled and burned.

She shook her head in disgust at both herself and him. "I said take me home. Then get out of our lives."

"I'll take you home. And I'll get out. But out of what life? You call what you have here a life?"

He turned the key in the ignition, and the engine growled, then purred. He put it into gear and began to back down the weedy drive. Gina combed her fingers through her hair, struggling to erase all evidence of contact with Connor Munroe. His handkerchief had fallen to the floor, and she let it lie there. She would not touch it.

Refusing to speak to him, she bit her lip and stared at the cannery again. The air around it seemed to swarm with ghosts, mocking her. Once, Loren's father had worked there. So had Loren, for five summers. Her own father had, as well. And Gary Orsini and Curtis Bates, and a horde of other lively people. Gone now, all of them.

"I said I was sorry," Connor muttered. "But before I leave, you'd better listen to one thing I came to say—and that's about selling to Beekman."

Incensed at the mention of Beekman's name, she sat more stiffly and kept her gaze turned away.

"Only a fool doesn't listen when money's being discussed."

She pretended she hadn't heard him.

"I get it," Connor said sarcastically. "The silent treatment. How original. How mature."

She ignored him. She leaned her elbow on the door, put her chin in her hand and gazed up at the moon. Stupid moon, she thought, stupid, hypnotic, lunatic moon. It had made her crazy. Or the stars had. Or the memories. She didn't know. All she wanted was the safety of home, of her bedroom with its hundred reminders of Loren.

The cannery's drive was rutted and rough, and the MG bucked as Connor backed it out to the highway. Gina endured the bumps as stoically as a cowboy on a bronco, still not speaking. She would never speak to him again. She hated him.

He swung the little car onto the road and hit the gas. It started down the moonlit road, but it was still bucking and swaying. Connor swore. Gina flashed him a suspicious look, then her thoughts went back to resenting the stars and moon.

The car's engine hummed quietly, but from somewhere beneath the car came an ominous sound. *Thuggudy-thuggudy-thug*, groaned the sound. *Thuggedy-thug.*

Connor swore again, more vehemently. "Damn! It's the tire. I don't bloody believe this." He swung the car over to the shoulder of the road. It came to a stop in a billowing cloud of gravel and dust.

Connor swung his long body out of the car, slamming the door viciously behind him. Gina watched him, her jaw set as angrily as his. She'd recognized the familiar limp of the car and the sound, as well: a flat tire, its flabbiness thudding against the highway.

She, too, got out. She, too, slammed the door unceremoniously. She stormed to where he stood, staring down. The rim of the wheel was flat against the gravel. He shook his head and the light streaks in his hair glinted.

"I suppose you planned this, too," Gina said, crossing her arms militantly. "Just so I'd have to listen to what you'd say. Well, don't say it. Don't say a word. Just be quiet, change that tire, and get me home. And if you try to touch me again, I . . . I'll pick up a rock and hit you smack upside the head."

He stalked back to the door, snatched the keys from the ignition and limped to the car's trunk. "I didn't plan it. I intend to change the tire. I'll talk all I want—and I'd rather be hit on the head with a rock than touch you again. Touching you is like touching poison ivy. It just starts trouble."

He pulled out a peculiar instrument from the trunk, thrust it under the bumper and began to twist the handle. Gina had never seen such an odd tool, and it made her suspicious. "What is that?"

"A jack," he said acidly, turning the handle harder.

"I never saw a jack like that."

"It's a big world. It's full of lots of things you never saw."

Gina tossed her head. "You'd just better have a good spare tire," she said. "Or you'll be sorry." She straightened her faded T-shirt, as if the motion could lend her additional dignity.

He eyed her chest with ironic interest. She wasn't sure if he was staring at her breasts or reading the shirt's message—"Ladies' Sewing Circle and Terrorist Society."

"That's a mighty appropriate T-shirt," he muttered, taking the spare from the trunk. "You should have a whole closetful. Knowing you, you probably do."

"What's that supposed to mean?" she demanded. "That I probably do?"

He examined the spare in the moonlight, then leaned it against the bumper. "As much as you hate change," he replied with false pleasantness, "you should just wear the same thing every day. Like what's-his-name—Jughead in the comic strip."

"Don't you dare call me a jughead."

He straightened, spread his legs slightly and put one hand on his hip. It was a dangerous stance. "I didn't call you a jughead. 'Terrorist' is a lot more accurate. Although 'temptress' could fit, too."

"Temptress? Me? A temptress? I went out to clean toilets tonight to avoid you, you egocentric fiend."

"Yeah," he sneered. "Shaking your cute little bottom and showing two miles of legs. And always saying, 'Don't touch me, don't touch me.' Then you hammer and pound on a man so much he *has* to touch you in self-defense—"

"Oh," gasped Gina. "You make the truth twist like a snake. I told you not to talk. Just be quiet and hurry up."

"And I told you I'll talk all I want. I'll recite all the capitals of Europe and the Middle East. I'll sing Broadway show tunes if I want, starting with 'Why can't a woman be more like a man?'"

And he did. In his husky, slightly off-key baritone he began a song that said women's heads were full of rags, cotton and hay.

Gina threw her arms down rigid by her sides, her fists clenched. "Beast!" she cried. "I'll walk."

He sang on, in praise of the male sex, its honesty, nobility and fairness.

Infuriated, she gave the skinny jack a kick for emphasis, then whirled away and marched off down the moon-drenched highway that led to Allegro and home.

From behind her came the sound of metal sliding against gravel, a sickening thud, then silence. Connor's satiric song suddenly stopped, ripped off in midnote. She heard a long, sinister intake of breath, the sound of a man steeling himself against pain.

For a moment, the sounds didn't register; then her stomach wrenched in apprehension. She stopped, spinning to face the car again. Horrified, she saw Connor sinking awkwardly to one knee, his other leg stretched out, his foot pinned by the fallen car.

Even as she watched, his body dropped lower, as if the ground were sucking him down. He crumpled and lay beside the car, writhing but soundless. He struck the earth with his fist, in anguish or in rage, she wasn't sure which, and she thought he swore, but the pain in his voice swallowed up the word.

Blood drained from her face. *He's pinned under the car,* she thought sickly. *I kicked the jack, and now he's pinned under the car....*

She ran and fell on her knees beside him. His teeth gritted in a grimace, his eyes were squeezed shut, and once more his clenched fist impotently struck at the earth. Every muscle in his body seemed tense with agony.

"Mr. Munroe," she begged, gripping his shoulder in terrified sympathy. "Connor, I'm sorry, I'm sorry."

He writhed again, as if cringing from her touch. "Don't be sorry," he said between his teeth. "Get the damn thing off me."

Numbly, blindly, Gina rose, her knees stinging from the gravel. Time spun drunkenly in her head, going both too swiftly and too slowly. She retrieved the jack and struggled with its strangeness. Eternity seemed to pass before she could get it into place and correctly twist the unfamiliar handle. She kept twisting and, a torturous fraction of an inch at a time, the car rose.

Her hands shook, and she feared she would knock the jack out of place again, pinning Connor even more. But at last the car was levered high enough so that the wheel was off his foot.

She heard him suppress another gasp of pain as he pulled free. He rolled a few inches farther from the car, then lay still, panting, half-coiled into a knot, only his injured leg straight.

Once more Gina ran to him, dropping to her knees, then sinking to half lie beside him, so she could cradle his head in her arms, keeping his face from pressing against the stones. He groaned slightly and twisted, as if to escape her touch.

She wriggled into a position that allowed her to force him to rest his head in her lap. His teeth still ground together, and he kept his eyes tightly closed. She ran her hand frantically over his forehead and was dismayed to find it clammy.

He grabbed her elbow, squeezing so hard she gasped. But intuitively she realized he grasped her not out of anger, but out of pain—it was so great, he had to hang on to something. She kept stroking his forehead and babbling words of comfort.

Panic spread through her, hectic as fever. How badly was he hurt? Mere bruises couldn't cause such pain. He must have sprained or broken something—and the fault was hers.

Suddenly, with a sigh of surprising gentleness, the rigidness in his face faded into exhausted peace, and he went limp in her arms. His hand fell away from her elbow and landed, a deadweight against the gravel.

Oh, Lord, I've killed him, she thought, paralyzed by fright. Could a man die from having a car fall on his foot?

A blood clot traveling from the leg to the brain could kill a person, she knew. Had one killed him?

Then, with stomach-wrenching force, she remembered something that until now had registered only on the periphery of her mind. Connor had a limp. Had something terrible once happened to his leg? Had she, in a stupid moment of rage, aggravated an old injury that threatened his health, his very life?

"Please don't die," she whispered fiercely, hugging him more tightly. She glanced about frantically for help. There was none. The road was deserted. The stars shone down just as uncaring and merry as before; the moon looked on as complacently.

"Please don't die," she repeated, even more fervently. "Please. I'll do anything if you just won't die."

She could have wept with relief when his eyelashes finally began to flutter, their shadows playing darkly on his pale face. Anxiously she stroked his hair away from his forehead. One of his eyebrows jerked almost imperceptibly into a frown. The corner of his handsome mouth twitched downward.

Gina held her breath. "Mr. Munroe?" Her voice shook with concern.

He exhaled sharply, a sigh of pain or resignation, she couldn't tell. He didn't open his eyes. "Gina?" he said. "Is that you strangling me?"

Immediately she loosened her grip, but she still held him, afraid to let go. She had an eerie irrational fear that if she didn't keep hold, his spirit might slip away completely, ascend and disappear behind the clouds of stars.

"Are you all right?" she breathed. "How badly are you hurt?"

His eyes still closed, he frowned harder. "I've felt ... better." He grimaced again.

Gina's heart shriveled with guilt. She bit her lip and shook her head remorsefully.

"Gina?" he said between his teeth. "I'm going to ask you a question."

"Yes?"

"It's the most important question I've ever asked a woman."

She didn't understand, but agreed, if only to humor him. "Yes?" she said, resisting the impulse to smooth his hair back from his brow again.

He opened one eye and stared up at her, squinting against the dazzle of star shine. "Will you let me go," he asked, "and go change the bloody tire? You've got a lovely lap, but I don't want to lie all night in it."

LATER SHE COULD barely remember how she'd changed the tire or the details of the drive to the emergency ward in Milledgeville. What she remembered most clearly was her struggle to help him to his feet, or rather foot. He had to wind his arm around her neck, then lean on her to hop painfully to the passenger's seat. He was a big man, and she almost buckled when he inadvertently put all his weight on her.

She wrapped one arm around his torso to help support him, and her face was unavoidably pressed against his chest. Grit from the shoulder of the road clung to his shirt, scratching her cheek. Through the ruined garment she felt the hardness and heat of his body.

She asked him if she should take off his shoe and see how bad his foot was. He leaned back against the seat, his face screwed up in torment, and shook his head vehemently. "You don't want to see it. It's a mess."

Gina didn't argue. She ran to the driver's side, got in, then drove as fast as she could to Milledgeville Hospital. All she knew was that the drive was rough; she was not used to a gearshift, and the little car rattled and jumped in protest more than once.

Connor kept swearing softly, "Damn, damn, damn." Gina didn't know if he was swearing at his pain or at her driving.

She refused to leave his side when they reached the emergency ward. He protested when two orderlies put him on a gurney, he protested when she came with him to the examination room, and he protested when she told the doctor on duty she intended to stay—that she was the person responsible for his injuries.

The doctor, obviously tired, grumpily said, "Suit yourself," then told Connor to be quiet; the nurse was trying to take his blood pressure. The doctor, whose name was Fonsby, cut away the shoe. Trained as he was, he winced at the sight that greeted him.

Gina flinched and turned away, feeling faint. Connor's foot was bruised and swollen, but that was not what stunned her. What shocked her was the number of scars, both pale and angry red, that snaked about the foot as if it had been stitched together from scraps, like Frankenstein's monster.

"Good grief, man," she heard Fonsby mutter. "What in the name of all that's holy did you *do?*"

"Boating accident," Connor said between his teeth.

Fonsby whistled. "Some accident."

"Yeah. In the hospital, they called me 'Dances with Outboard Motors.'"

"You're lucky to still dance with anything," Fonsby said. "Does this hurt?"

"Like very hell," Connor said with a sharp gasp, and Gina, ashamed, flinched again and kept looking away.

"Get her out of here," Connor said pointedly, and she knew he meant her. "She looks green."

"It might be a good idea," Fonsby agreed as Gina sank into a chair, covering her eyes with her hand.

"CHEER UP. You didn't kill him," Fonsby said several endless hours later. Gina now sat in the emergency ward waiting room, in the same guilty pose, slumped in the chair, her elbow on its arm, her hand over her eyes.

"What?" she asked numbly, dropping her hand and blinking up at him without comprehension.

"You didn't kill him," Fonsby repeated. "What's the matter? Did you want to?"

"Of course not. Will he be all right?"

Fonsby sighed and adjusted his glasses. "If he's lucky. And if he follows orders. He doesn't seem the type who likes to follow orders."

"He's not."

"Well," Fonsby said, studying her sternly, "you're going to have to make him."

Gina's eyes widened in surprise. "Me?"

Fonsby nodded. "You. He said he was staying with you and your great-aunt."

"Well, he *was*—" Gina began.

Fonsby, a busy man as well as a tired one, cut her off. "I'm remanding him to your care."

"But—"

"Keep him off that foot and in bed as much as possible. I want to see him in another couple of days. The X rays show nothing's broken. He's exceptionally fortunate. But the old injuries have been traumatized, and he shouldn't take any chances. He also threw his knee out of joint. That's extremely painful, but it's back in place. It shouldn't give him any trouble. Keep ice packs on the foot for the first twenty-four hours. Then if the pain persists, use a heating pad."

Gina only stared at him. Unsmiling, Fonsby stared back. "You're lucky you didn't do more damage than you did. I never saw such a set of scars in my life. He needs *very* good care. Understand?"

Guilt closed around her like a thick cloud. She had committed the deadly sin of anger, and now she must pay for it.

Her punishment was that Connor would stay in the house, and she would have to wait on him like a bond servant.

She swallowed hard and nodded.

"Good," Fonsby said. "Now take him home."

"Take me to a motel," Connor ordered as soon as she started the MG. He sat with his leg sticking out at an awkward-looking angle, his foot swathed in gauze and bandages. A set of rented crutches had been thrust into the tiny back seat.

She tossed him a loaded glance. "I can't. You're supposed to have care."

"*He* thinks so," Connor muttered, nodding back in the direction of the emergency ward. "I can take care of myself."

"You told him you were staying with us."

"So he wouldn't slam me into the hospital. Now, take me to a motel."

"You're supposed to stay in bed with an ice pack."

"Oh. And you're the ice pack?"

Gina set her jaw and gave him a resentful sideways glance. "It was just that kind of talk that put you into the emergency ward in the first place."

"So what will you do this time? Drop a semi-truck on me?"

She took a deep breath, willing herself to be patient. As she passed the Holiday Inn at the edge of Milledgeville, her fingers tightened on the wheel. In a few seconds she would turn off the main highway and take the exit to Allegro.

"Turn around. Take me to the Holiday Inn."

She straightened her back, raised her chin and took the exit. "No. You've already paid to stay with us. And you need care, bed rest. I suppose it's the least I can do."

"No. The least you could do is apologize."

She lifted one shoulder in a guilty shrug. "Of course. It goes without saying."

He lifted one brow in unamused irony. "It certainly has till now. Turn around and take me to that motel."

"No. You'll fall down the stairs trying to get to the ice machine. You'll call room service, and when it comes, you'll trip trying to get to the door and kill yourself. Who knows what could happen?"

"What a compendium of disasters you are. I mean that in every way."

Gina forced herself to ignore his contrariness. "Besides, I'm supposed to take you back to the doctor in two days. You can't drive."

"I'll use my left foot."

"You'd have an accident. No."

Connor swore.

"Look," Gina said, darting him a determined look, "I owe this to you, all right? It's my fault you're hurt, so I owe it to you. I don't like it any better than you do."

"You insist, eh?"

"Yes. I insist." She bit her lower lip.

"I see."

He leaned back and looked up at the stars as if in resignation. He said nothing else. The night wind tossed his hair, and he shook his head as if something amused him.

Gina was grateful for his silence. How was she going to explain this whole complex mess to Earline? *He lied to us, so I tried to break his foot off. I did a better job than I intended.*

Suddenly he laughed. The sound made Gina shiver, even though the night was warm. Then he was silent again, as if savoring something.

"I'm not a pleasant patient," he said, still staring at the sky.

"I can tell."

He smiled slightly. "I can turn your life into living hell."

She gripped the wheel more tightly. "I have no doubt."

Smiling, he turned his face toward her. She didn't like the smugness of his smile one bit. "Why are you grinning at me like a Cheshire cat? Stop it."

"I'm contemplating the irony. You wanted to stalk off and leave me. You wanted to kick me out of your house. Instead, you're driving me there yourself, my personal chauffeur. And you're going to wait on me. Hand and—you'll excuse the expression—foot."

"I don't see the humor," Gina said darkly.

"I do. First, you'll have to give me your bedroom. I can't negotiate stairs. I'll not only be in your house. I'll be in your bed. How'll you like that?"

"It means nothing. A bed's a bed." Her heart knocked uneasily against her ribs. They had entered Allegro, which seemed to doze in the night. The streetlights cast a gentle glow over its sleep.

"But in your bed how can I help having carnal thoughts about you?"

"I'm not interested in your thoughts. I'm not interested in anything about you."

"And you'll have to listen to more of my thoughts about Beekman's offer. I've got you now. You're my captive audience."

"I'm not interested in Beekman, either."

"Which bothers you more? The carnal thoughts—or that I'm on a mission for Beekman?"

"Neither," she said with a carelessness she didn't feel. "Because neither one makes any difference. I won't even think about them."

"What if I make you think about them?"

Her mouth was dry. She shrugged.

He watched her. "When you kicked that jack, you thought it was like kicking a door shut—that everything was over. But it's not. Instead, you kicked a door open." The smile faded from his face. "We've just begun, you and I. Just begun."

She pulled into the driveway and turned off the ignition. The living room lamp was on, its light falling softly through the window onto the porch. There was a beat of silence, then the crickets started to sing.

It all seems so peaceful, she thought unhappily. *But there can't be any peace with him under the roof.*

"Don't brood, Gina." His voice was low, husky. "You brought it on yourself. And you said it yourself—you owe me."

She turned to him. The shadows fell so that they masked all of his face except for those cool startling eyes of his. "You can't change my mind about anything," she said, shaking her head.

The eyes flicked up and down her body. "We'll see about that," he said.

CHAPTER SEVEN

EARLINE WAS APPALLED when she heard the story. "I've been waiting up hours for you two, worried sick," she said. "Now I don't know which of you to be most disgusted with. Really!"

But Gina knew with whom Earline was most displeased. The sight of Connor hobbling on crutches immediately earned him Earline's sympathy. Gina had been lied to, but she looked more guilty than injured and seemed no worse for wear. Connor, obviously damaged and in pain, appeared far more grievously wronged.

Earline fumed and bustled, helping Gina move Connor into Gina's downstairs bedroom. She clucked in dismay as she helped pack Connor's foot in ice. Then, still fuming and bustling, she helped Gina carry her things to the upstairs room vacated by Connor.

"Really, Gina!" she said, as soon as the door closed. "So the man wasn't altogether honest—you didn't have to drop a *car* on him."

"It was a small car," Gina said miserably. "And a big lie."

"So he lied," Earline muttered, angrily stacking Gina's clothing on the bureau top. "That's no excuse to put him in the emergency ward. A lie is only words. 'Sticks and stones may break my bones, but words will never hurt me.' You're lucky you didn't kill him."

Gina stared at her in consternation. Earline, bundled into her old bathrobe, looked as if every nerve in her body was vibrating. She was badly rattled, and her mood, Gina could tell, was volatile.

"Earline," she pleaded, "he weaseled his way into this house. He deceived us. Please don't take his side."

Earline put her hands on her hips. "I'm not taking anybody's side. You're both in the wrong. Everything always goes crazy at festival time—everything. But at least you never tried to commit mayhem before. *Mama mia,* why do we put ourselves through this madness? What's wrong with us?"

Gina, who had been turning down the bedclothes, stopped. She stared warily at her aunt. "Oh, no. It's started—your festival nerves. What's happened?"

Earline tossed her head. "You mean in addition to you? Mary Ellen Orsini called. She's got measles—measles! So *I* have to supervise making the spaghetti sauce—all week long. As if I didn't have enough to do. I've still got four naked elephants downstairs—four! Naked as jaybirds. Now there's an invalid in the house. And—"

"Earline, calm down," Gina said. "*I'll* take care of him. It's my fault, so…"

Earline shook her finger at Gina and dropped her voice to a dramatic whisper. "We'd just better both take excellent care of him, miss. I don't know how else we can make up for doing such a terrible thing."

"We?" Gina asked, bewildered. "You didn't do it. It's not your fault."

"I raised you. It's on my head, may heaven forgive me." Earline crossed herself, then clasped her hands. "What if there are complications? What if he never walks again?"

"He'll walk again." Gina put her hands on Earline's shoulders, trying to calm her. "The doctor practically assured me of that. All we have to do is see that he takes it easy and rests—"

"Then in this house he rests like a king," Earline vowed. "Heaven forbid it should be any worse than it is. Promise me, Gina. You promise me that. No matter what your differences with this man, in this house he rests like a king.''

Earline was growing more upset by the minute, and Gina knew better than to argue. ''Shh,'' she soothed. She took a deep breath, hoping the words she was about to utter wouldn't cause heaven to strike her dead. ''Shh. Yes. In this house, he'll be treated like a...a king. I'll make it up to him. I promise.''

She bent and kissed Earline's cheek. She gave her aunt's shoulders an encouraging squeeze. ''Now go to bed. Don't worry. Everything will be fine.''

At last Earline trundled off, muttering prayers under her breath. Gina, exhausted, shut off the light and fell across the bed, not bothering to change her clothes or get under the covers.

She buried her face in the clean crispness of the pillowcase, as if she could somehow find refuge in its folds. But a subtle hint of Connor's cologne clung to the fabric, haunting it like a ghost.

Connor. I don't want to think of him. It's wrong to think of him.

Yet she couldn't help herself. Her body now lay on the very spot where he'd lounged that afternoon, powerful and sure of himself. The memory of his presence tingled through her.

She tried to will the tingles away, but they wouldn't go. How had everything gotten so crazy? she wondered. How had everything turned so upside down?

Now he was lying in *her* room, his big body violating the intimate privacy of *her* bed. In the room's darkness, half a hundred snapshots and souvenirs of Loren surrounded him like a guard, while she was alone, unprotected by all her comforting reminders. It wasn't right. Nothing about this night had been right.

Agitated, she pushed the pillow away and rolled onto her back, one arm behind her head to cushion it. She let her

other hand rise to her lips and touched them tentatively.
They still burned from Connor's touch, and the memory of
his mouth against hers sent a shuddering pang through her.

I didn't like it, she told herself, remembering his kiss. *I
didn't like it. I hated it.*

She kept saying it to herself over and over, until she almost believed it. Only then could she sleep.

CONNOR THOUGHT it would take all his charm, a lot of work
and a great deal of luck, as well, to win the aunt back to his
side. He was pleased to discover he was wrong.

Earline was up at dawn, peeking in on him, seeing if he
needed anything. She brought fresh ice for his aching foot,
then she scampered back to the kitchen, filling the house
with the fragrance of baking biscuits and perking coffee.

The scents mingled with those of the spice field, which
came through the open bedroom window. The spice field
stretched behind the house, like a large, slightly untidy yard.
He could see it from where he lay.

Earline brought him a tray bearing a feast of scrambled
eggs, ham, orange juice, butter, four kinds of jam, biscuits
still steaming from the oven and hot coffee. A pink rose,
picked from the vine on the front porch perhaps, was thrust
into a vase. A drop of dew still glittered on its petals.

He asked Earline to sit by his bedside because he wanted
to talk to her. He apologized profusely for having lied to her
and Gina. He had come partly for Gina's own good, he said;
he didn't think Gina yet understood how much money might
be at stake for her.

Earline accepted the apologies even more profusely than
he gave them. She confessed that in her heart of hearts, she
sometimes thought Gina might be better off giving the recipe to Beekman. The festival was such a nerve-racking af-
fair, how long could the people of Allegro keep it up?

Connor commended her on both her insight and open-
mindedness. He asked Earline questions about Allegro, the

festival and especially about Gina. She was only too glad to tell him everything he wanted to know.

When she reached to take the tray away, Connor put his large hand over her small one. "We got off to a bad start." He smiled. "It feels better now that everything's out in the open. Thank you for forgiving me, Earline. You're lovely women, you and Gina both."

Earline blushed and got as twittery as a bird. She almost fluttered upstairs to wake Gina, whom she had let sleep late.

Connor leaned back against the banked pillows and smiled to himself, feeling like a cat who has just eaten one canary and now planned to dine on one he thought even more delicious. How easy it was to beguile these women. All he had to do was tell the truth. What could be simpler?

AWAKENED, GINA SAT UP in bed, rubbing the sleep from her eyes, disoriented to find herself in the guest room.

"Go shower. Clean up. Do something with your hair," Earline fussed. "Hurry. I have to go to the parish hall. He's being just wonderful about all this. Don't put on another pair of those awful cutoffs. Put on a dress. Stay close to him in case he needs anything."

When Earline finally dithered off to the parish hall, Gina felt almost giddy with relief. She heard the front door slam, footsteps patter down the porch stairs and the crunch of gravel as Earline backed the car out of the drive. Gina sighed, then stared at her reflection in the dresser mirror.

She had a pale green towel wrapped around her torso and a pink one around her wet hair. From downstairs she heard faint strains of music. Earline must have taken her radio into Connor's room.

Gina switched the guest room radio on to drown out Connor's music and create her own private world of sound. Tina Turner was singing "We Don't Need Another Hero."

Indeed we don't, Gina thought rebelliously. She used to dress up and try to look pretty for Loren. She didn't do that sort of thing anymore. Earline might grumble and fret, but Gina refused to give up all her principles.

She slipped into another pair of cutoffs and a baggy old short-sleeved pink shirt. For shoes she chose her least elaborate, a pair of blue rubber thongs. As for fixing her hair, she toweled it dry, gave it a few halfhearted brushes, and pinned it back at her nape with a barrette. From there, she decided, it could style itself.

She applied a touch of pink lipstick only because her lips looked unnaturally pale. Then she tied her baggy shirt in a knot at the front and strolled downstairs, her head high and her pace casual. Her thongs went flip-flop, flip-flop against the carpeted steps.

She followed the scent of coffee into the kitchen and poured herself a cup, steaming and black. She slathered half a biscuit with cherry jam and was about to sit at the kitchen table when a deep male voice summoned her.

"Gina? Are you having coffee? Have it in here. I'm bored."

Bored, Gina thought, rolling her eyes heavenward. Earline hadn't been out of the house five minutes, and he was bored. What was she supposed to do with him all day? Put on puppet shows and tap-dance for him?

Carrying her cup and her biscuit, she sauntered out of the kitchen, through the hall and to Connor's room. Despite her lazy pace, her heart knocked unaccountably hard against her breastbone, and she realized her muscles were tensed into knots.

Nonsense, she told herself. Why be tense? He was only an ordinary man, not even a nice one. He was, for example, devious, and that was only the first in the long list of his flaws.

She stepped inside the bedroom doorway and stared at him without speaking. Even though she kept her face as blank as possible, her thoughts seemed to spin suddenly out of control.

No matter what she said about him, Connor Munroe certainly didn't *look* like an ordinary man sitting there, leaning against the white wicker headboard of her bed. The morning sunlight poured through the window, gilding his rumpled hair. And she'd been wrong about his eyes—they were far more electric and far bluer than Earline's morning glories. As always when her gaze met his, a shock, half pleasurable, half frightening, rippled through her.

A wry smile curled the corner of his mouth. "Wow. Am I flattered. You really gussied yourself up for me, didn't you?"

"No." Gina took the last bite of her biscuit and chewed it slowly. She looked about the room because she didn't like looking at Connor. It was a bit like looking at the sun; he made everything else go dim.

"Join me." He patted the edge of the chair that Earline had so recently occupied. "Keep me company?"

She didn't move. "Is that a request?" she asked, eyeing her bulletin board. "Or a command?"

"Which does it take?"

Gina shrugged and moved to the chair. She sat, putting her cup on the bedside table, leaned back, and precisely crossed her long legs at the ankles. "And how is our foot this morning?" she asked. "Do we feel better?"

"Good Lord," he said, "when I was unconscious, did you drag me off and marry me?"

Gina recoiled. "Of course not!"

"Then what's this 'we' business? You talk as if we're one flesh or something. We're not. It's my flesh that's throbbing, not yours."

Chastened, Gina gave him a wary glance. He wore a short-sleeved knit shirt of peacock blue, and his jaw was clean-shaven. Earline must have helped him out of his old shirt and into a fresh one; maybe she had even shaved him. Someone had to help him with such things. Tomorrow she might be the one. Troubled by the image of touching him so intimately, Gina had to look away from him again.

He was too big for this room, she thought in helpless perplexity, too broad of shoulder, too wide of chest. He was too blond, too powerful, too dangerously full of energy. He didn't belong in this little room with its delicate white furniture. It was like trying to imprison a lion in a wicker bird cage.

"Your foot," she said, nodding at the sheet that covered his lower body. "I suppose it still hurts."

"You suppose correctly."

She shook her head in regret. "I'm sorry. That's...bad."

"No. It's good."

When she glanced at him this time, his eyes caught hers and held them. "Why...why is it good?" she breathed.

He no longer smiled. He studied her face, his own solemn. "It's better than feeling nothing. It can be a good sign, pain."

"I'm sorry. About the pain, I mean."

He folded his arms and shrugged. "If that's the price, that's the price."

"The price of what?"

"Of starting over. Now we start over, you and I. At least, I hope so. Will you let it happen?"

Gina shook her head. "There's nothing to start over. But I am sorry—about your foot, I mean."

His gaze stayed locked on hers. "Are you? Really?"

"Really."

"Why? Because I'd be gone by now if you hadn't caused this 'little accident'?"

She made a small futile gesture. "Partly."

"Only partly," he said, raising one brow. "What else might you regret?"

She shrugged and stared down at her nearly bare feet. She suddenly wished she'd taken a little more trouble with her clothes. She felt like a ragamuffin.

She took a quavering breath because all of last night's guilt came edging back, as strong and gloomy as before. "I truly regret that I caused you . . . suffering. I regret that— hurting you."

"I hurt you, too. And Earline. By lying. She forgave me. Will you?"

Gina kept staring at her feet. She wiggled her toes and shrugged again. Then she raised her head and looked about the room at the dozens of reminders of Loren.

She concentrated on Loren's portrait on her dresser, as if it was an object of meditation that might focus her mind.

Connor spoke again, his voice intent. "I lied for the sake of business. It's not something I usually do. I don't like myself much for doing it."

"Business," she said tonelessly.

"Business," he repeated. "In personal matters I never lie to women. I tell them the truth."

She drummed her fingertips against her tanned thighs and kept her eyes on the portrait. "What *is* the truth about you?"

He was silent a moment. Then he spoke, seeming to pick his words carefully. "The truth is this—I'm a man who's just passing through. I don't linger. But when I look back on this, I want the memories to be good. For both of us. And to know that you forgave me. I'm asking again—will you?"

She stared so hard at Loren's picture that its edges began to blur. She took a deep breath. "I'm not sure it's a question of forgiveness. It's more a question of being even. I went too far, trying to get even. Now I'm paying for it."

He gave a soft, cynical-sounding whistle. "You keep strict accounts, Gina."

"Yes," she said, "I do. Listen, this really isn't getting us anywhere. Do you mind if I go?"

She started to rise, but his answer was swift, the tone unrelenting. "Yes, I mind. Beekman sent me here, and I was ready to walk away, give it up. But now I have to stay—because of you. I want to talk to you. That's all."

She settled back into the chair, recrossed her legs and let one foot joggle nervously. She crossed her arms, too, as if to protect herself. Once more she stared at Loren's picture. *Loren, Loren, Loren,* she thought. *I love you. I always will.*

Connor's voice cut across her consciousness like a blade. "Gina," he said softly. "Don't look so unhappy. I just want to be friends. Maybe the Man Upstairs was sending me a message when you kicked that jack. Maybe he was telling me that lying to you was a lousy thing to do. That I'd better tell the truth from here on out. What do you think?"

She refused to meet his gaze. "I don't have an opinion on what God thinks. Are you going to try to talk to me about Beekman again?"

"I think you both would profit from this deal. That's the truth. But that's not what I want to talk about. I want to talk about you."

She heard him shift on the bed. From the corner of her eye, she could see that now he leaned across the bed toward her, his weight on one elbow. The position would be painful, she thought, because he'd have to move his foot; the blood would go pounding through it in new and painful ways. The thought made her nip guiltily at the inside of her cheek.

"Gina, will you look at me? What's the matter? Are you frightened? Here—give me your hand." He stretched his toward her.

She sat more stiffly on the chair, clenching her fists into balls. "No."

"Gina," he said, his voice seductively soft, "are you afraid even to touch me? Is that it?"

She swallowed. "Of course not."

"Then take my hand. For just a minute. While I tell you something. Something...hard for me to say. Don't be afraid. Please."

She turned to face him, her chin defiantly high. "Why should I be afraid of you?"

He stretched his hand closer. His mouth had a determined crook to one corner. She knew his position was costing him pain, but he refused to give in to it. "Just hold my hand. If nothing else, to show you don't hate me."

"Stop reaching. You'll hurt yourself."

"Then it'll be your fault."

He reached farther still, and she could tell that he wouldn't retreat. With an impatient sigh, she placed her hand in his. "There," she said gruffly. "I don't hate you— exactly. Now lie back."

He gave her a crooked smile and leaned back to rest against the pillows stacked against the headboard. The smile flickered away into a rictus of pain as he straightened his leg again. His fingers tightened their grip on hers until the twinge passed.

"Look," he said, studying her face, "I'm sorry I lied. But I'm even sorrier about...the other. For kissing you. I didn't understand."

She tried to draw her hand away, but he held it fast. His thumb began to move slowly over her knuckles, a gentle sensuous motion.

He stared at the ceiling as if hoping it might reveal the right words. After a moment he gave a short, self-mocking laugh. "I said this would be hard. I didn't know how hard. Here goes. I figured it out. I'm the first one. Since him. Right?"

She stiffened, feeling as if someone had poured ice into her backbone. "What?"

He lowered his gaze to the bulletin board on the opposite wall, frowning slightly. "I'm the first one who's kissed you. Since him." He nodded at the myriad snapshots and souvenirs of Loren.

"Oh" was all she could say. Now she felt as if the ice in her spine was spilling into her arm, chilling her captured hand into numbness against the warmth of his.

He turned and gave her an unreadable look. "You feel guilty. Don't. It was my fault. All mine. All right?"

"Oh." The sound, helpless and hopeless, seemed the only one she could utter. She shook her head in confusion.

"I tried to blame you. That was wrong. Nobody blames a rose for being beautiful. I repeat, the fault was mine. You have nothing to feel guilty about. Understand?"

She bit her lip and nodded. Once more she tried to draw her hand away, but still he kept it imprisoned. "No," he murmured. "There's more. Your aunt says you've stayed faithful to him. For six years. That's a long time."

He paused awkwardly before he spoke again. His thumb caressed the cool flesh of her inner wrist. "Maybe it's time you let yourself be kissed again. You're very...kissable, Gina. Very desirable. There's no sin in that. None."

She sat staring at him, her body as rigid as if she'd been hypnotized. Her breath felt frozen in her lungs.

He kept his eyes trained on hers. "You remind me of a princess in a fairy tale, Gina. A spell's been cast on you. And you lie caught in that spell, protected by your fortress. This town is your fortress."

She reached deep inside herself for words. "This town—"

"Shh," he said. "Listen. Just a moment longer. In stories, the spell can be broken by a kiss. Not just any kiss— the *right* kiss. Mine wasn't right. I'm sorry. But don't blame a man for trying. It was hard to see you in the moonlight and not try."

Gina looked away again, her face hot and cold at the same time, her heart stammering in confusion.

"Someone will kiss you into life again," he said, holding her hand more tightly. "I wish it had been me. I envy that man, whoever he is. But I'm nobody's prince, Gina. Certainly not yours. And for that, I apologize profoundly."

He raised her hand to his lips and kissed it. His lips felt vital, warm and silky against her cold knuckles. Then he smiled his crooked smile and released her hand. "But maybe we can be friends. Can we have that, at least?"

She drew back from him as swiftly as if he were a fire. Wordlessly she rose and gazed down at him, her breathing still choked. Her hands clenched and unclenched at her sides.

"That was," she said in a tight voice, "the worst baloney I've ever heard in my life. I should have dropped that car on your *head*."

Disbelief flashed in Connor's eyes, then anger. "What?" He straightened mutinously against the headboard and glared at her.

"You heard me," she said, tossing her curls. "That was nothing but unmitigated tripe. You tried to butter me up like a . . . a piece of toast."

"What?" This time he almost roared.

Gina didn't flinch, but only narrowed her eyes. "If you want that recipe—which you'll *never* get, by the way—you'll have to do better than that. A princess in a fairy tale—hoo, boy. Break the spell with a kiss—spare me, please. Why don't you grow an oily little mustache and prowl cruise ships to romance rich widows? *Really.*"

Connor was not used to women reacting so, and he found the image of himself as a cruise-ship gigolo particularly galling. His mouth turned down in a bitter smile. "You think I said all that for a stinking bunch of spices?"

"Yes." She put her hands on her hips and nodded. "I do."

He gave her the same peculiar bitter smile. "Did it occur to you that I might mean it?"

"Not for a moment."

"You don't think I have a sincere bone in my body, do you?"

"No. Not one. Except maybe the bruised ones." She gave a curt nod at his foot. "I suppose they're sincerely bruised."

"Yeah," he said sarcastically. "They're really most sincerely bruised. Look, I went out of my way trying to communicate with you. You want me to say the same thing plain, instead of fancy?"

"However you put it, it's hooey."

"Hooey," he said with distaste. He folded his arms militantly across his chest. "I pour my heart out, and she calls it 'hooey.' All right. I'll say the same thing with no frills. You're pretty. Why don't you fix your hair? Put your lipstick on straight? Why don't you wear something tighter than a circus tent?"

"For you?" she said with contempt.

"For anybody. Your problem is you're afraid somebody'll notice you're a woman. Look at you. Look at this room."

"Nothing's wrong with my room," she retorted, "except that you're in it."

He made a gesture of disdain. "It's not a bedroom—it's a damn shrine. You live like a nun. Except instead of religion, you've been worshiping a dead man for six years. A dead man—and a dying town."

"It's not a dying town."

"The buzzards are circling. If you had the courage to take your head out of the sand and look up, you'd see them."

"I *loved* Loren," she said angrily, distressed to find herself once more on the verge of tears. "I always will."

"He's dead," Connor said with cruel frankness. "I told you—you love a dead man."

"There's nothing wrong with that."

The sarcastic smile faded from his face. His blue eyes grew scornful. "Yes, there is, Gina. There's something really wrong about loving a dead man—he can't love you back.''

She stiffened as though he had slapped her. ''He was worth a hundred of you,'' she said between her teeth. Then she turned her back on him and walked from the room.

Connor glared after her, resentment seething. Had he been too flowery when he talked to her? Had he gotten carried away? Maybe the dizzying scent of the spice field had somehow made him go too far. But, dammit, at the moment he was saying it, he'd have sworn he meant every word.

She *was* like a princess frozen by a spell. He would like to kiss her back to life. Not for himself, but for her own sake. Somewhere out there was a prince for her, if she'd only bother to wake up and take a look.

But no. She was the most hardheaded, wrongheaded woman he'd ever met. He'd tried to handle her gently, but he might as well have tried his kindness on a piranha.

''Get yourself a life, Calvino,'' he yelled after her, his tone scathing. ''And I *am* sorry I kissed you. Next time I get the urge, I'll kiss a band saw.''

Only silence answered him.

He didn't call to her again. She did not return to his room. He didn't see her again until almost noon, when he tried to hop, swearing and using one crutch, into the kitchen for fresh ice.

That was when he fell.

CHAPTER EIGHT

CONNOR WAS CONSCIOUS of a fresh surge of pain ripping through his foot, and he was conscious of hitting the floor, twisting so that his shoulder took the blow's force.

The next thing he knew, Gina was crouched by his side, her hand on his arm, her brown eyes enormous with fright. He was vaguely aware that she'd changed the baggy shirt for something yellow and formfitting, and that her lipstick was now on straight.

Mostly, however, he was aware of feeling like a fool as he lay half in and half out of the kitchen, hurting like the very devil.

"Ouf," he said inelegantly as he tried to rise.

"*Now* what have you done to yourself?" she asked, pushing him so that he lay with his back on the floor. "Have you hurt your foot even more?"

"My pride more than anything."

"Why did you get up?" she demanded. "You're supposed to rest."

"I needed ice," he said, rising on his elbows again.

"You never called. You should have called me."

"You never came in," he countered. "For all I knew, you were gone."

"Here," Gina ordered, "put your arm around my shoulders. I've got you. I'll help you up. How did you do this to yourself?"

"An elephant," Connor snarled between his teeth. "I tripped over a bloody elephant."

Gina glanced at an elephant sitting in its underwear on the kitchen floor, waiting for Earline to finish its costume.

"You should watch where you're going," she scolded, winding her arm around his waist.

"He ambushed me." Connor scowled malevolently at the stuffed animal. "A man doesn't expect elephants underfoot in the kitchen."

"Well," Gina said, helping to hoist him up, "she runs out of room, that's all."

Connor was upright again, balancing awkwardly on his good foot and leaning against Gina. She was tall, but slim, and he leaned on her so hard he was afraid his weight would drive her into the floor like a nail.

"Give me my crutch. Let me get my ice and get out of here."

"No," Gina said, gritting her teeth in determination. "Get back in that bed right now."

Grudgingly Connor kept leaning on her and let her lead him to the bedroom. He lowered himself onto the mattress, then drew his breath in pain as he positioned his feet. Loose-fitting khaki shorts did little to cover his long legs, which were roped with sinew and glinting with dark gold hair.

Gina tried to ignore all his blondness and muscle, even though her shoulders still tingled from his weight. "Now lie down and get under the sheet," she ordered, "and I'll get your ice."

"I don't want to lie down. I don't want to get under the sheet. I feel like a cadaver."

"Then let me plump your pillows. Look, do you want a book or something?"

"My pillows are plump enough. And yeah, I'd like a book. Nice of you to ask after I've spent the morning staring at the walls. And what does it take to get lunch around here? A Supreme Court ruling?"

"My," Gina said, stepping back and smoothing her hair. "We're in a grouchy mood, aren't we?"

"No, we are not. *I* am." He glared at her from beneath his forelock of blond hair. "Why shouldn't I be? I've been hit by my own car, starved in mind and body and bush-whacked by an elephant. What's to be cheerful about? That an asteroid hasn't landed on me?"

Gina tried to hide the smile that teased at her lips. "Are you sure your foot's all right?"

"Yes. It's my foot, so I ought to know. It's my shoulder you've done in this time." He put his hand to his shoulder, then drew it back, swearing. Blood tinged his fingertips.

Gina's smile died and her stomach made a sickening loop-the-loop. "Blood? What's wrong?"

"You've whittled at my legs. Now you're starting on my arms." He swore again, twisting his head in an effort to see the injury to his shoulder.

"*I* didn't do anything. You did it to yourself," Gina said righteously. "Here. Take your shirt off. Let's see."

He shot her a suspicious glare. "I'll take my own shirt off. You'll strangle me in it."

He whipped the shirt off over his head, then tried again to see how badly he was hurt.

Without thinking, Gina went to him, sitting on the edge of the bed and putting her hand on his back. "Here. You can't see. Let me."

He went peculiarly still at her touch, looking over his shoulder at her. Quickly Gina dropped her gaze to the back of his right shoulder. A new bruise was emerging on the muscles, and a spot of bronzed skin was scraped raw.

She touched it self-consciously. His flesh twitched slightly beneath her fingertips, as if in response. She became all too conscious that he had a wide beautiful back that tapered to a narrow waist.

She'd glimpsed his bare chest, as well, and it, too, had disconcerted her. A sheen of curling golden hair covered it like a breastplate. So much blondness seemed foreign to her, handsome, but alien and perhaps dangerous.

She sat, holding her breath, barely touching him, for the space of two heartbeats, then three.

"Well?" he challenged.

Drawing back her hand, she inched imperceptibly toward the edge of the bed. She realized that a drop of his blood shone on her fingertips. "Another bruise. And a scrape. You'll live."

"I was afraid of that."

"I'll get the first-aid kit."

"Wait."

There was such authority in his voice that she raised her eyes and met the fierce blue of his. As always, that dark-lashed gaze jolted her, leaving her feeling weak and empty.

"You're wearing perfume." His voice was so low it was somewhere between a purr and a snarl. It gave her a shivery vulnerable feeling between her shoulder blades.

She tried to shrug nonchalantly. "So?"

He didn't answer. His gaze lowered to her mouth and dwelt there. Involuntarily she sucked in her breath.

"I'll get the first-aid kit," she repeated in a small voice. She rose quickly and left the room, the haunting scent of the spice field wafting through the window, following in her wake.

When she returned, he had once more put up his facade of irony and ill-temper. She breathed a secret sigh of relief and erected a facade of her own. Aloofly she cleaned his scraped shoulder, trying not to notice the sleek planes of his back.

He demanded another shirt. She was grateful to step to the closet, choose one at random and toss it carelessly to him, staring out the window while he shrugged into it.

As he buttoned his shirt, he complained of hunger. She informed him he'd be fed as soon as humanly possible, then turned haughtily and left the room.

She brought him lunch on a tray, a ham-and-cheese sandwich on Earline's homemade bread, the last of the

brownies and a glass of iced tea garnished with mint from
the garden.

She also brought him a copy of the novel *Great Expectations,* which was almost four hundred pages long, and told
him she hoped it would help pass the afternoon.

"Sit," he ordered, gesturing at the chair. He held out half
the sandwich. "Take this. I never see you eat. It makes me
nervous. What if you pass out? I'll have to get up again, and
Lord knows how that might end. In my death, probably."

She resisted, but finally gave in to his cajoling. She found
that behind their combative exchanges, once in a while they
were starting to smile at each other, almost shyly. Conversation became a game they played, and as they played it, she
slowly began to like it.

"So why," he asked, his mouth sardonic, "does Earline
have all these elephants? Why just elephants? Why not once
in a while an ostrich or a kangaroo rat?"

Gina shrugged. "Even she doesn't know. She just says she
likes elephants. They make her feel peaceful."

He cocked an eyebrow. "I see. So tell me why no two are
alike. Wouldn't it be easier to dress them all the same?"

"That's the point," she said. "If she made them alike, it
would be boring. So she never makes two alike in the same
year. Or ever. If she made a ballet dancer last year and one
this year, they'd be different."

Connor frowned. "What if she had to make twins?"

"What?"

"If she decided to make twin elephants. Then she'd have
to make two alike. Or elephant triplets? Then she'd have to
make three. And quadruplets..."

Gina waved her hand for him to stop. "No. No twins or
triplets allowed. That's the rule."

"What rule?"

"Earline's rule. She makes the elephants, so she makes
the elephant rules."

His brow arched more dubiously. "Why doesn't she sell them through a shop during the year? A mail-order company or something. They're cute. She'd probably make money."

Gina shook her head. "A company might want fifteen of one kind. She'd never do that. Besides, if she took orders, then it'd be work, not fun. She might start to hate elephants. She only makes them for festival."

"I'm sure there's logic there somewhere. It just eludes me."

"My father called it Allegran logic. Once there was a woman at the cannery—Rose Alice—who knitted beautiful afghans. She made them for friends. Her neighbor, Calvert Paris, had a woodlot. He and Rose Alice didn't much like each other, and Calvert was famous for being tightfisted. But he wanted one of Rose Alice's afghans. He told her he'd trade her a load of wood for an afghan."

Connor finished the brownie. "Why do I have the feeling this story gets complicated?"

"Because it does." Gina smiled. "Well, Rose Alice wouldn't trade an afghan for wood because, then, making an afghan would be like work, not fun. So Calvert said he'd just give her money for an afghan, but she wouldn't do that, either."

"Same reason."

Gina nodded. "Right. Making an afghan to sell would be like work. So finally Calvert gave up. He drove a load of wood to Rose Alice's house and stacked it, all nice and neat. 'Consider it a gift,' he said. And you have to remember that Calvert never gave anything away—ever.

"Rose Alice said, 'Why, isn't that thoughtful of you, Calvert! You've never done anything like that before.' And because he'd been so generous, she made him an afghan and tied it up with a ribbon. Every year after that Calvert gave Rose Alice a load of wood. And every year she made him an afghan or a sweater or something nice in return." Gina paused and laughed in nostalgia. "They never did get to like each other much, but they kept it up, that gift giving, for years."

Connor scowled. "But they were trading—why not be honest about it?"

"No," Gina disagreed, "they weren't trading. Rose Alice refused to. Every afghan was a labor of love. She wouldn't make what she did into something, you know, commercial. So every year she and Calvert exchanged gifts. It was rather lovely, really."

Connor shook his head. "It makes no sense."

Gina's dreamy smile faded. She put the half of the sandwich back on the tray, untasted. "It made sense in Allegro," she said softly. "It made perfect sense. I didn't suppose you'd understand."

"Gina—"

"No," she said, brushing imaginary crumbs from her lap. "It's like Beekman."

Connor's face went uncharacteristically somber. "Let's not talk about Beekman. Let's declare a moratorium on the subject."

"No," she insisted. "I have to make you see this. If Beekman had the festival, it wouldn't be a labor of love anymore. It would just be something people did for the money in it. And then it wouldn't mean the same thing."

She stood. "I'd better get to work. Call if you need anything." She gave him a wan smile. "Don't go skating on elephants again."

He looked her up and down with an odd measuring expression, as if seeing her for the first time. "Don't go," he said.

She blinked in surprise. "What?"

"Don't go. Stay with me."

Unsettled, she shook her head. "No. I can't. Wesley's coming over. I promised to crochet a harness for his frog."

"Let the frog crochet its own harness. It gets lonely here, Gina. I'm not a man who takes easily to idleness."

"Read your book," she said. "Play the radio."

"I'm not the radio type. And I've read this book. More than once, in fact."

"I'll get you another."

"I don't want another. I want you."

The words 'I want you,' spoken so matter-of-factly, made her skin prickle. She looked away from him, disconcerted.

"I mean," he said, voice low, "I want you to stay. We can talk. Play cards. Anything. This isn't a pleasant room to be alone in."

She let her gaze flick about the room, settling on first one reminder of Loren, then another. "I like it."

"I don't. You know what memento mori means?"

She had been staring at Loren's college portrait on her dresser. Guiltily she looked away. "Yes. It means a reminder of death. A symbol of death."

"That's what this room is like when you're gone. Nothing except reminders of what's dead and gone. I've heard saints were supposed to contemplate memento mori, to remind them of eternity. I'm no saint, Gina."

Her mouth took on a bitter quirk. "No. You're not."

He picked up the book and held it toward her. "It's odd that of all books you could have brought, you brought this one. Have you read it?"

Her cheeks began to burn. She knew what he was about to say. "A long time ago."

"You remember the character Miss Havisham?"

Gina's cheeks tingled more fiercely. "Nobody forgets Miss Havisham."

"Shut away in her decaying room," Connor persisted, "in her decaying house. An old woman in a yellowed bridal gown and a tattered veil, obsessed about a groom who was gone. All her clocks stopped forever, and her cake rotted and covered with cobwebs."

Gina threw him a hot resentful glance. "I'm *not* living in my wedding gown. I *don't* keep a cake in this room. Time hasn't stopped for me. Miss Havisham was a bitter, empty old woman. I'm not Miss Havisham."

"Good," Connor said, his blue gaze steady. "Don't become her. It would be a shame for a woman like you."

She tilted her head at a defiant angle, her chin set. "You know nothing about me. You're...you're presumptuous and...and insolent, that's what."

"Then stay and humble me," he taunted.

Gina flung her head even higher and turned on her heel. "I'll humble you, all right," she muttered. Then she stalked away, leaving him alone. Half a hundred pictures of Loren stared down at him, as if in derision.

Connor swore. "Come back, you coward," he called after her. But she did not come back.

WESLEY DEAN PARIS came over at one o'clock to visit his frog. He picked it up and tucked it under his arm. "Why's that man still here?" he demanded. "You didn't go to your shop this morning. Why not?"

Wesley Dean's little gray eyes were so beady with curiosity that Gina blushed. "The man hurt himself."

Wesley's expression brightened. "Did he hurt himself bad?"

"Bad enough," Gina said. "He can't walk."

"Wow!" Wesley said happily, "Did he break his leg? Bad? It serves him right. He interrupted our fight."

"Gina?" Connor's voice boomed from the bedroom. "Is that kid here? Are you deserting me for a child and a frog, for God's sake?"

Agitated, Gina pushed her curls back from her forehead and tried to concentrate on Wesley. "No. His leg isn't broken."

"Gina!" Connor's voice was a low resentful roar. "At least bring me another book."

"He yells a lot," Wesley said, looking righteous. "My mother says you shouldn't yell in the house."

"Your mother's right." She put one hand on Wesley's plump shoulder and led him to the dining room table where her workbasket sat. "Let me measure your frog, then I'll make his harness."

"I want a red harness," Wesley said. "Has Earline got any brownies left?"

"No. The man ate the last one."

Wesley cast a hostile look in the direction of the bedroom. "Is he in *your* room? Your bed? Why?"

"So he doesn't have to go up the stairs on crutches. Give me your frog."

Wesley handed the frog over, and Gina measured it gingerly with her tape measure. "Does Earline have any cookies?" Wesley asked.

"I don't think so. She'll bake again when the festival's over."

"That's another week," Wesley complained, wiping his glasses on his T-shirt. "I'll starve."

"The boredom is killing me, Gina," Connor shouted. "This is cruel and unusual punishment. I hope that *child* spreads it all over the neighborhood—you're killing me with boredom."

Gina bit her lip. She handed the frog back to Wesley. He stood, the frog in his hands, staring malevolently in the direction of Connor's voice. "What a party poop," he said.

Gina sat at the table and made a loop of red crochet thread. She tensed her shoulders in anticipation of hearing Connor's next complaint.

Suddenly inspiration struck her as palpably as a physical blow. She sat back in her chair and gave Wesley a crooked smile. "Wesley Dean, would you like to earn some money?"

Wesley's eyes glittered at the thought. "Doing what?"

"Well," Gina said, her smile growing more crooked, "call it baby-sitting. The man, you see, gets bored. I'll pay you seventy-five cents an hour to keep him company and to fetch and carry for him."

"Make it a dollar," Wesley said firmly.

"Consider it yours," said Gina with satisfaction. She sat back to crochet in peace.

CONNOR WAS ANNOYED to see Wesley Dean standing in the doorway, staring at him and clutching a large green bullfrog. He glowered at the boy. "What do you want?"

"I'm your official baby-sitter," Wesley Dean said with a superior air. "Do you want to play Monopoly? Nobody can beat me at Monopoly, not even Gina."

Connor crossed his arms and stared at the ceiling in disgust. "I don't believe this. No, I don't want to play Monopoly."

Wesley picked up Gina's unfinished sandwich half. "You want this?"

"Not after you've had your froggy little fingers on it," grumbled Connor.

"Here, hold my frog, will you?" Wesley asked, thrusting the frog upon him, then sat down to eat the sandwich.

Connor stared at the frog with repugnance. "What's its name?"

Wesley took a large bite and studied Connor as he chewed. "What's *your* name?" he demanded, his mouth still full.

"Mr. Munroe," Connor said, glowering down at the frog, which was large and moist.

Wesley gave a smile in which Connor perceived evil in its purest form. "Then that's his name, too," Wesley informed him. "Mr. Munroe, the slimy old bullfrog."

"How nice," Connor muttered, not amused. "Remind me if I ever have a warthog to name it Wesley Dean."

Wesley Dean belched loudly in reply.

EARLINE CAME HOME exhausted after a full day of supervising the making of the festival sauce. Wesley left, hopping behind his harnessed frog. Earline sat down at the kitchen table with a weary sigh and watched as Gina arranged a tray for Connor. "You eat with him, dear," she said. "I'm too tired even to talk. And he must get bored in there."

"I don't want to eat with him."

"Gina," Earline said, a warning note in her voice, "you promised me—in this house . . ."

"I know, I know," Gina said restlessly. "In this house, he'll be treated like a king. It's just that after a full day of him, His Majesty's getting on my nerves."

Earline shot her a severe look. "And whose fault is it that he's *in* that bed, eh, miss? Oh, I'm so tired, I may fall asleep right in this chair. And another two days of this, then the festival, and me with all those naked elephants. Oh, I swear, it's not worth it, it's not worth it—we're all mad to do it. Why did I ever discourage you from selling that recipe? It'd be a favor to us all. . . ."

Gina swept up the tray and made for Connor's room as quickly as she could. Earline was going into one of her negative moods, and even Connor would be easier to face.

He looked at her sourly when she entered. "What have you done now? Put ground glass in my food?"

Gina smiled sweetly and set the tray on his lap. "Have you washed the frog off your hands? Or should I bring you a washcloth?"

"I can totter to the bathroom quite nicely, thank you. What did you pay that weevil to sit with me?"

"Wesley isn't a weevil," she said, perching primly on the edge of the chair.

"He's an evil demon-child from the darkest pit of hell. And he cheats at Monopoly."

"Really? I hadn't noticed. I'm Miss Havisham, remember. I just sit and watch my wedding cake rot. It takes all my attention."

He sighed harshly. "All right. I'm sorry about the Miss Havisham remark. But you've got to admit, it was an odd book to bring when I'm trapped in a room like this." He nodded with irritation toward her bulletin board, laden with its snapshots of Loren.

"I knew a woman like her once," he said. "Her name was Fanny Mercator. She was the sister of...a good friend of mine. I'd hate to see you end up like her, that's all."

Gina said nothing. Perhaps she had reacted so strongly to his accusation about Miss Havisham because there was a germ of truth in it. She no longer knew.

"I'll take the pictures upstairs," she said, her voice resigned. "All the other things, too. You won't have to look at them."

"But you will."

"I like looking at them," she murmured, gazing at the bulletin board.

"Then why's your face so sad?"

Gina was tired of jousting with him. "Maybe because you're here and he's not."

Connor raised one brow sardonically. "*Touché*. Excellent shot, Gina. Did you use your pretty little razor-blade tongue to put *him* in his place, too?"

She folded her arms and stared coolly at Connor. "There was never any need. His place was by my side, and mine was by his."

"How touching."

She smiled slightly, her mouth scornful. "I doubt if much of anything touches you. What is it, anyway, that makes you talk like this? Will Beekman fire you if you don't get the spices? Too bad, because you're not getting them."

He gave a short laugh and set his tray on the bedside table. He settled back against the banked pillows and stared at her. "Beekman can't fire me. I don't work for him. I work for myself. I own *American Vagabond*. The whole Vagabond chain. But what happens to those spices—if I don't get them?"

"Answer me first. What's Beekman got that you want? Something made you cross half a continent to annoy me. And eat. You're supposed to keep your strength up."

"My strength is fine, thanks. Would you care to test it?"

Although he made no move toward her, she took an involuntary step backward. "No. And you're avoiding the question. What's Beekman got that you want?"

He reached toward the tray, took one olive and popped it into his mouth. Then he crossed his arms and gave her a tight slanted smile. "A yacht."

"A boat?" Gina said, half amused, half appalled. "You're going through all this for a measly boat? You're even shallower than I thought."

"She's hardly measly. And I want her. And there are a few more besides her."

Gina cocked her head derisively. "You *want* her. And to get her, you'll ride roughshod over anything or anybody. Including me. And this whole town."

He nodded toward his injured foot, bound up in its towel full of ice. "I'm not riding roughshod. I'm not even moving, dammit. Now, what about my question? What happens to that recipe if Beekman doesn't get it? Do you take the secret to your grave? What's supposed to happen to your precious festival then? Assuming—and it's a very chancy assumption—that this town still exists?"

Gina went to the wall and took down the bulletin board. She set it by the door, then began to gather other pictures and souvenirs from the bureau top, the dressing table. "When I die," she said without emotion, "I'll leave the recipe to the church—to this parish. Even if the town should become a part of Milledgeville, the church should still be here. The church can use the festival to raise funds."

Connor whistled softly. "I see. So my competition's God himself. No wonder I'm doing so badly. I almost sympathize with Beekman, the poor devil."

Gina cast him a cold stare. "Your sympathies have always been with the Devil. I'm sorry you won't get your boat. But there are other toys in the world. Hand me that teddy bear, please."

Connor glanced lazily at the teddy bear that lay on its back on the edge of the bed, next to the wall. "Another gift from the one and only Loren?"

"Yes. Hand it over, please."

He kept his arms crossed. He didn't move. He merely smiled. "You won't help me get my toy. Why should I help you get yours?"

"Oh, really," Gina almost snarled. Angrily she set her armload of souvenirs on the dressing table. She strode to the bed and reached across Connor's body for the bear. Just as her fingers closed over its plush leg, Connor pulled her against his chest.

"Gotcha," he said with satisfaction, looking down into her startled eyes.

Gina's heart leapt in alarm. She dropped the bear and placed both hands against Connor's chest, trying to force her way free. His half smile mocked her efforts, and he pulled her more tightly against him. His strong arms had easily shifted her so that she lay in his lap, her breasts crushed against the hardness of his body.

"Ah, Gina," he breathed, "if you could see the panic in your eyes. Am I the one you're scared of—or do you scare yourself? Are you afraid you're not as faithful to the past as you want to be?"

"Let go of me," she ordered.

"But it's so much easier to talk to you like this. I almost think you're listening."

"Let go," she repeated, beating her fist against his shoulder. "Let go, let go, let go."

"Listen to me. It's important. Beekman's willing to offer you a lot more money than you know. A great deal of money."

"I don't care about his money," she almost spat. She pounded on his shoulder again, although she might just as well have beaten on the wall.

"Shh," Connor almost hissed, bending his face nearer hers. "I said listen. I've been thinking all afternoon. Take his money, Gina—but ask for more still. Ask him for a percentage of his profits when he markets the sauce. Try for four percent, but settle for two if you have to. You'll be set for the rest of your life. You'll never have to worry about money again."

"I don't," she raged, "care about the stinking money! There's more to life than money—can't you understand that?"

"I understand all too well," he muttered. "I'm talking about that, too. It's one thing to deny yourself the money. It's another thing to deny . . ."

He paused, his arms holding her even more tightly. His eyes, troubled and fiery, held hers. "It may even be a sin to deny yourself this—"

He lowered his mouth to hers and kissed her.

"Or this," he breathed against her parted lips, then kissed her again.

CHAPTER NINE

AT FIRST GINA STRUGGLED, but such tides of conflict surged through her that she finally lay still in Connor's arms, neither resisting nor responding. She simply tasted and felt the strangeness of so intimate a touch.

She sensed power in the hunger of his kiss, a power so elemental that it shook her to heart and swept her, helpless, into its current.

He awoke a turmoil of light and darkness within her. Stars and moons and comets seemed fall in showers all around, dizzying and disorienting her. Her hands trembled to rise and lock behind Connor's neck, as if only his strength could keep her from dying in tides of unconsciousness.

But to touch him only brightened the white flame of desire within her. Softly she opened her lips beneath his and let his tongue enter the sanctuary of her mouth. Years of loneliness and denial bloomed into yearning as his kiss deepened.

All day she had secretly remembered the exciting muscularity of his arms, how tightly, how securely he could hold her. In secret she had recalled how his lips could commandeer hers, lighting a vital spark that set her body ablaze.

He drew back, and her eyes fluttered open in confusion. He stared down at her until the intensity of his gaze seemed to penetrate her very soul. "What I can't believe," he breathed, lowering his lips to hers again, "is that I apologized for doing this."

"This—" he nibbled at her lower lip "—needs—" his tongue traced the curve of her upper lip "—doing." He kissed her so thoroughly that once again she saw meteors raining through the darkness.

"This needs doing very much," he growled against the smoothness of her cheek. He trailed kisses along her jaw and pressed them against the throbbing pulse in her throat. "This needs doing again—" he nuzzled the silky line of her shoulder "—and again and again."

He raised his lips to hover, poised, above hers. His breath tingled against her vulnerable mouth.

"Kiss me," he ordered, his voice husky. "Kiss me back."

Slowly, almost reluctantly, Gina lifted her mouth to his. She settled her lips against his, at first softly, then with greater urgency as her longing swelled.

Her need fed and fanned the fire of his. With a rough sigh, he swept her down to lie beside him as his hands explored the planes of her back, pressing her body more firmly to his. Gina gave a little cry and clung to him, dizzied by the force of her emotions.

"Gina? Gina?" Earline's voice echoed down the hall. "Lindy Marchesi's on the phone. She wants to know if you have the robes and the crowns for the festival princesses and queen. You do, don't you? At the shop?"

Startled and suddenly ashamed, Gina almost sprang from Connor's arms, but he held her fast. "Tell her you'll call back," he said. "Then close the door. Does it lock?"

Gina could only stare at him, her heart beating so hard that it hurt. His mouth was set at a determined, almost cruel angle, and it was slightly smeared with the faint remains of her lipstick. His gaze seemed as blue as the heart of a flame to her.

She raised herself slightly and called to Earline. "Earline? Tell Lindy I'll call her back. All right?" Her voice sounded strange and stiff with false cheerfulness.

"Good," Connor said, drawing her down and kissing her again. "Now lock the door."

He let her slip from his arms, and she rose, moving quickly toward the door. When she reached it, she paused, then stared back at him with true panic on her face.

He rose on his elbow. "Gina—don't leave," he said, a frown line forming between his brows.

She took several deep and ragged breaths. The pungent scent of the spice field seemed to overwhelm her, make her feel half-drugged. She shook her head in frustration and self-disgust. "I can't do this," she said. Her voice shook. "I *won't* do this."

He sat up, bending his good leg and resting his arm on it. It was a posture both casual and dangerous, full of coiled energy ready to spring. He stared at her, challenge in his eyes. "You want to do it. Deny it, and you're lying."

"No."

"You're lying."

"Gina?" Earline's voice, slightly querulous, called again. "Have you seen that old rhinestone brooch I set out? I need it for my elephant princess."

Gina opened the bedroom door and her frightened gaze flicked down the hall. She was relieved to see it was empty. "It's on the mantel in the living room," she called, her voice tight. She turned and gave Connor a look she hoped was cold.

"Eat your supper," she said. "I told you, you need to keep your strength up."

"And I told you. My strength is fine. It's not food I'm hungry for."

"Then I can't help you."

"Can't you?"

"No."

"Come back to me. Tonight. After Earline's asleep."

"No." The word felt almost torn from her. She spun out of the room and ran up the stairs. Her heart still beat too hard and ached so sharply that she wondered if heaven was about to rend it, striking her dead for her sins.

She dashed into the guest room, flinging the door shut behind her. Then she sat on the edge of the bed and buried her face in her hands. But she could not cry. She could only sit there, her heart pounding like a wound, her throat choked.

Then she realized that she had dropped all her souvenirs of Loren back in Connor's room. It was as if she'd first defiled them, then deserted them. She bit her lip. She had even let Connor kiss her and lie beside her, while Loren's bear was tossed thoughtlessly aside on the same bed, forgotten. What kind of a woman was she?

The tears came, hot and furious, and she silently sobbed until her throat tore with it and her ribs ached.

THE EVENING BREEZE stirred the curtains, brought a stronger aroma of growing spices into the room. Connor frowned. He was growing to hate the scent. It stirred unwanted and unsatisfied hungers in him.

"You haven't eaten anything," Earline said, concerned. "What's the matter?"

Moodily Connor fingered the worn copy of *Great Expectations*. "I'm not hungry, thanks."

Earline picked up the untouched tray. "I'll put it in the refrigerator. I can heat it up later if you're hungry." She paused and frowned. "Where's Gina? Why's she taken down all Loren's pictures?"

Connor set the book aside. "She went upstairs. She meant to take the pictures with her."

"Oh. She'll be back, then."

Connor didn't think so. Gina had been too badly shaken. He felt off balance himself. At the time, kissing her had seemed the right thing to do, had seemed inevitable. After all, he'd lain all day in this damnable bed thinking of her. A chemistry strong enough to explode existed between them. He couldn't deny it, and neither, he knew, could she.

But if kissing her had been right in one way, it was wrong in a thousand others. He supposed she was upstairs crying her eyes out, and the thought gave him a cold, nasty knot in the pit of his stomach.

Earline, not noticing his somber mood, was humming. She shrugged and took the tray away. She returned a few moments later carrying an elephant and an armful of organdy spangled with sequins. "Do you want company?" she asked.

"Sure," Connor said without true enthusiasm. Earline sat down and shook out the organdy. It was a gown, and she fitted it on the elephant.

Connor watched her. Her face looked tired, her complexion gray, but her manner was as animated as ever.

"I wish Gina would take those pictures down and keep them down," she confided, fluffing the elephant's skirts. "I don't think it's good for her, frankly."

Connor stared at the bulletin board, brooding.

"Loren was an exceptional young man," Earline said, threading a needle. "But she can't devote her life to him. She needs to get on with her own. I think she's quite an attractive young woman. Do you?"

The knot in Connor's stomach jerked tighter. "Yes. You could say she's attractive."

"Personally," Earline continued, "I don't think she'll ever find anyone to suit her in Allegro. Why, she never could even see any of those other boys for Loren. And most of them are married now or gone away. She needs to widen her horizons, if you ask me."

"Right," muttered Connor.

"Loren would want her to. He was that sort of person."

"What was he—some sort of god returned to earth?" Connor asked sarcastically. He'd looked at too many pictures of Loren, heard his name too many times, felt as if

Loren was an unwanted entity, dwelling in this room, breathing his cold ghost's breath down Connor's live and human back.

Earline took no offense. "Well, Gina certainly thought of him that way. He was...good. He was the most sincere person I ever knew. Serious. A homebody. Devoted to his parents and family. And to Gina. Oh, there was never anyone in the world for him but Gina. She could always make him laugh, you know."

Connor settled more deeply into his bad mood. He knew that he himself was seldom sincere; he was usually flippant or sarcastic. No one would ever accuse him of being serious. He believed in three things only: freedom, making money, and moving on.

He was the farthest thing from a homebody anyone could imagine. He was devoted to nobody except himself. There had been women before Gina, and he imagined there would be women after her.

He knew that Gina could make him laugh, but his talent seemed to consist of making her cry. He was, in short, as unlike the saintly Loren as possible.

"Now you say," Earline said, darting him a measuring glance, "that you're not married. Would it be too personal to ask if you're...involved with anybody?"

"I don't get involved," he said grimly. He took a deck of cards from the night table and began to play solitaire. The stupid teddy bear, still tossed and lying on its side, seemed to watch him with bright, disapproving eyes.

"So there's no one you're going home to?" Earline asked a bit too casually. "Back in California?"

"There's nobody. And no home to go to," he said, still dealing. "California's just temporary."

"I see. So where do you go next?"

He dealt the jack of diamonds. "The Caribbean, maybe. I'm thinking of starting a charter business."

"Isn't that fascinating?" Earline said, eyeing him thoughtfully. "You know, Gina and I have never been anywhere like that. Neither of us has ever even seen an ocean. I think she should see a bit of the world while she's still young. More than this little town, anyway. Don't you?"

"It's a big world," Connor said between clenched teeth. "And a small town. Yeah. She should get out."

"The thing that worries me," Earline said, "is there's no future left in Allegro. Everything's passed us by. We'll either dry up and blow away, or Milledgeville will absorb us. Either way, it means an end to Allegro."

"Everything ends," Connor said, turning up the ace of spades.

Earline shrugged philosophically. "So they say. Well, I'm prepared to face it, but Gina certainly won't."

She set a tiara on the elephant's head and began to stitch it into place. "But I'm rattling on too much about us. What about you? Do you suppose you'll ever settle down?"

Connor suppressed a sigh of exasperation. Earline was checking him out as potential husband material, and none too subtly. His game had reached a dead end, so he gathered the cards back together and expertly shuffled them, like a gambler. It was a trick Fred Mercator had taught him. "No. I'll never settle down. It's not in my blood."

Then, because Earline looked so clearly disappointed, he added with gruff gallantry, "But if I were the settling type, I'd settle with someone like her. Your niece, I mean."

He wasn't sure when he said it if it was a lie or not.

GINA APPEARED at the doorway half an hour later. Her face was free of makeup, and he knew she'd scrubbed it to wash away all trace of tears. He knew, as well, that the absence of makeup was a message for him—*I'm not trying to attract you. I don't want to.*

She stood very straight, and her beautiful smile seemed strained. "I'm going to my shop," she told Earline. "Lindy needs the robes. She wants to air them out before the festival.''

"A good thing," Earline said, not looking up from her sewing. "Last year when they crowned the queen, moths flew out of her robe. The effect was hardly royal."

Gina studiously avoided looking at Connor. "But first I'll put these things away." She picked up her bulletin board. Nervously she walked to the bed, her spine still ramrod straight, and thrust her hand out. "Would you give me that bear, please?"

Connor thought she blushed. The last time she'd asked for the bear, she'd ended up in the bed with him, instead. He kept his gaze locked on her purposely expressionless face, but she still didn't meet his eyes.

"My pleasure," he said. He picked up the bear and handed it to her. She took it without thanking him, turned and awkwardly scooped up the rest of the souvenirs from the dressing table, then left the room.

"I wish she'd get rid of that bear," Earline whispered when Gina went back upstairs. "Loren gave it to her for her sixteenth birthday. It's getting moths of its own. Besides, she's too big now to sleep with teddy bears."

The knot in Connor twisted harder. He looked at the empty doorway. "I know," he said.

ACT NORMAL. *Act as if nothing ever happened,* Gina told herself the next morning as she paused outside Connor's door. Once more Earline had risen early and served him breakfast. But now Earline was gone, it was still too early for Wesley Dean to appear, and Gina was once more alone in the house with Connor.

She knocked briskly on the doorframe, then stepped just inside the room. "Earline's gone," she said without smiling. "I'll be in the kitchen packing the last of the spices. If you need anything, please call. I don't want a replay of that fall you took yesterday."

She barely glanced at him as she spoke, but even that small stolen look jarred her so much her nerve ends tingled. His electric blue gaze was as disconcerting as ever, his sarcastic half smile as disturbing.

His dark blond hair hung in a thick lock over his forehead and curled at his neck where it was long. It gleamed gold in the sunlight falling through the windows. He wore a snow-white T-shirt and cutoff jeans. His injured foot was wrapped in Earline's heating pad.

Slowly he raised his hand to his brow in the parody of a salute. "Yes, *sir,*" he said out of the side of his mouth.

Gina stiffened her back. She, too, wore cutoffs, along with a man's work shirt, pale blue and baggy. On her feet were her most disreputable running shoes. Once again her face was bare of makeup. She'd pulled her hair back into a careless glossy ponytail of curls. She wanted to look and feel sexless.

"I repeat, if you want anything, call," she said, all business. "I'll take you to your doctor's appointment at ten forty-five. Then we'll come back, and I'll give you lunch. After that, I turn you over to Wesley."

"The hell you will," retorted Connor. "He reminds me of that fat little kid in the Addams Family. The one who plays with guillotines and crocodiles."

"He's a lonely little boy," Gina said, setting her chin at a righteous angle. "And his father's in the hospital recovering from a heart attack. It won't kill you to be nice to him."

"It might."

"I'm sure there's no such luck," she answered with false sweetness. "So unless you need me, I'll see you at about twenty after ten to drive you to the doctor. Any questions?"

He crossed his arms and leaned back against the pillows. "Yeah. I've got a question."

"What?" She almost snapped the word, so impatient was she to escape.

He nodded, his eyes traveling up and down her body. "Are you going into town wearing that?"

Offended, she shot him a sharp look. "I dress to please myself."

"You're easily pleased." He gave her his most disgusted smirk. "Why don't you just wear a potato sack? Rub ashes into your hair? By the way, none of it works. You still look good. And you'd probably look good in a potato sack, too."

"Will there be anything else?"

"Yes. This morning I'm not going to grovel and ask forgiveness for kissing you. I liked it, and so did you. So put that in your pipe and smoke it, Calvino. And stop pretending you've transcended biology."

She stared at him a long smoldering moment. "The only thing that gives me any pleasure at *all* having you in this house is that you're never going to get my recipe—or your precious boat. You'll have to go home without it."

He cocked an eyebrow and smirked more crookedly. "But the boat was to *be* home. Without it, there's nowhere to go. I'll just have to stay till I get it, won't I?"

"That," Gina said with spirit, "will be when hell freezes over."

"Whenever." Connor smiled.

"HE'S MENDING NICELY," the doctor told Gina in private. "He'll be able to get around with the crutches. But I don't want him putting any weight on that foot for a week. Don't even let him drive. If it starts paining him worse, make him get back in bed."

"Another week?" Gina asked, feeling slightly sick.

The doctor looked stern. "A week. Seven days."

She sighed, but the man paid her no notice.

"Bring him back in a week. And count your blessings. If he'd been hurt any worse, he'd be flirting with losing that foot. He almost lost it once, you know. Somebody less stubborn would have let them take it. Make him take care of himself, understand?''

The old guilt came flooding back to Gina, mixing with depression. ''I understand,'' she said in resignation.

They had taken the MG so that Earline could drive the other car to the parish hall. On the way home, the doctor's words kept gnawing at Gina's conscience. ''Did ... did you really almost lose your foot? When you had your ... accident?''

He sat with his elbow on the window's edge, his fist propped against his chin. He'd been somber since they'd left the doctor's office. ''Yeah.''

''I mean,'' Gina said, too ashamed to look at him, ''the doctor spoke as if you, well, came close to it.''

He shrugged one shoulder. ''*They* wanted to,'' he muttered. ''My opinion was different.''

She shifted uneasily in her seat. ''How long were you in the hospital?''

''Altogether? I lost count. Too long. Why? What's it to you?''

She cocked her head as if it was nothing to her at all. ''Just wondering. Where did it happen? California?''

''Spain.'' He turned to face her, the corner of his mouth twitching. ''What is this? Feeling guilty again? Good. You're nicer when you feel guilty.''

''Look,'' she said, making a helpless little gesture, ''you're so ... impossible, it's easy to forget how badly you might have been hurt. That's all.''

''It might have been bad, all right,'' he agreed. ''You could have undone a year's healing. A damned hard year, too. I'm lucky you didn't make me an amputee, after all.''

Gina cringed at the word and set her teeth.

''You *should* flinch,'' he mocked. ''And you should try to make it up to me.''

She grimaced. ''I *have* tried. I'm trying.''

His eyebrow flicked up slightly as his gaze ran over her. "You did change clothes. I'll give you that."

She shrugged. She'd changed into a denim skirt, a yellow knit top and sandals. Because of his earlier sarcasm, she'd even brushed out her hair and grudgingly put on lipstick.

"Do you really want to do something nice for me?" he asked, a purr in his voice.

Her skin prickled. "It depends."

"Don't take me back to the house. Not yet. I feel like I'm in a cage. Drive around for a while. Show me this town you love so much."

Gina darted him a suspicious glance. "So you can make fun of it?"

"So I can see it through your eyes. Your—I might add—beautiful brown eyes."

Her hands clenched the wheel more tightly. "Only if you stop that," she said firmly.

He laughed at her. "Stop what?"

"Stop pretending to...to make love to me."

He laughed again. "Who's pretending?"

"You are," she said emphatically. "And I'm sick of it, because I know it's only for Beekman. So quit."

"What if it's not for Beekman? What if it's for me?"

She shot him another look, half warning, half wary. "Then you're wasting your time."

"It wasn't wasted. I enjoyed it. You did, too. Or would have, if you'd let yourself."

"See?" Gina demanded, shaking her forefinger at him. "There you go—that sort of remark. That's exactly what I want you to stop."

"Show me the town," he said with his derisive smile. "And maybe I will."

"All right," Gina said, as they approached the crest of a hill. "This is a tour of the places I like best."

"What's out here?" Connor grumbled, looking at the countryside. "There's nothing but fields and poultry houses."

"Yes, there is," she said with satisfaction as they topped the hill. She nodded forward and to their right. "There. How do you like that?"

Below them, in the valley, sat a small dilapidated farmhouse. Around it in every direction were fields. But they were not pastures or meadows or fields resting fallow between crops. There was acre after acre of brilliantly blooming flowers, seemingly millions of them, nodding in the sunshine.

Connor frowned. "What the . . . ?"

"Petunias," Gina said, taking satisfaction in his look of disbelief. "Forty acres of petunias. Smell them?"

She took a deep satisfied breath. She thought no flowers smelled more sweetly than petunias, and their scent was so thick and heady she felt intoxicated.

Connor looked out at the rainbow vista of flowers and nodded wryly, as if nothing after this would surprise him. "And what quaint rural madness is this, exactly?"

Gina gave him a wide triumphant smile. "It's Luke Caniglia's place. He's eighty-eight. But every spring, he climbs on a tractor almost as old as he is and plants petunias."

They passed the ramshackle house, which sat near the road. A round little man with a fringe of white hair sat in a rocking chair on the porch. He wore overalls and was smoking a corncob pipe. A yellow cat lay curled in his lap.

Gina stopped the car and honked. She raised herself so high in the seat she was nearly standing. She waved wildly. "Luke, Luke! Hi! It's me, Gina."

He smiled amiably and waved back, never missing a beat of his rocking.

"We could stop and talk to him," Gina said, settling in her seat again and stepping on the gas, "but he doesn't talk in August."

"What?" Connor craned his neck and looked back at the farmhouse.

"He doesn't talk in August," she repeated. "It's when his wife died. That's one way he shows he remembers. This—" she nodded at the flowers "—is another. There's a place up here we can stop. He put in a picnic table and some benches, so people can enjoy it."

They rounded a slight curve and Gina pulled the MG to a stop on a grassy verge. Edged by a picket fence, next to the tossing sea of flowers, was a neat little lawn as green as emerald. "Want to get out and look?"

"Sure," he said gruffly, and reached back for his crutches. She got out, walked to the edge of the flower field, closed her eyes and inhaled deeply. "Mmm," she said raptly.

Connor came, clambering up the slight incline to stand beside her. The breeze rose, ruffling their hair, swirling Gina's skirt behind her. She opened her eyes and gestured toward a small white marble monument set near the picket fence. Petunias, a pretty bed of them, grew at its base. The stone was engraved: "Tootie Caniglia, a Garden in Her Memory, with Love, from Luke."

Connor's face went expressionless as he read the words. He looked at Gina. "How long has she been dead?"

Gina looked up at him, her smile fading. "Twenty-eight years."

"Good Lord—twenty-eight *years*?"

She turned back to face the field of flowers again, smoothing her hair against the tossing of the breeze. "Twenty-eight years. He loved her very much."

Connor followed her gaze, staring out at the fields, a troubled line between his brows. "Forty acres?"

She nodded. "He had 320 acres once. But when Tootie died, he sold the rest. And all he's planted since are petunias. They were her favorite."

"And when he dies?" Connor, still frowning, studied the changing expressions on her face.

She clasped her hands together and shrugged. "I don't know. He and Tootie had no children. Relatives will divide it up, I suppose. I don't know if anybody'll want to farm it."

He was silent a moment, staring down at her. "So land developers from Milledgeville may get it in the end?"

Her face grew pensive. "Maybe. But not for a while. Luke's father lived to be a hundred and two, and Luke says he plans to do the same. And as long as he lives, this land is Tootie's garden."

Connor's voice was low, rough. "I see. And I suppose you've always come here. Since you were a little girl."

A phantom of a smile reappeared on her mouth. "In summer, my cousin Lucia and I would ride our bikes out here all the time. We'd bring our dolls and play. We could dress them in flowers." She gave a small rueful laugh. "And ants, too, sometimes. And we'd make ourselves dizzy on the flowers, looking, smelling, tasting them."

"Tasting them?" His eyebrow rose in skepticism.

"Yup." She bent, reached through the fence and picked two bright red petunias. Rising, she expertly removed and discarded the green stems of the blossoms. The blooms, with their delicately funneled shape, lay in her palm.

"Here," she said, carefully handing one to him. "Like this. You put the tiny end in your mouth—don't bite it—and just suck."

His eyebrow rose higher. "What?"

"Just do it," Gina urged. She raised the small end of the blossom to her lips, and Connor did the same, never taking his eyes off her.

She drew the nectar out of the flower, then smiled at him. "Did you taste it, the honey?"

Connor, taking the flower away from his mouth, kept his gaze still fixed on hers. "Yes."

"Every flower's like that. It has honey at the heart. Sweet."

Connor, his eyes bluer than the hot sky behind him, nodded. "Sweet," he said meditatively, looking at her lips. "Honey at the heart."

CHAPTER TEN

GINA LOOKED UP at the jeweled brightness of the stained-glass windows. "This," she said, "is the church where my parents, my grandparents and my great-grandparents were married."

Connor nodded wordlessly, moody again. *And where you would have been married,* he thought. What would she be like if she had gotten married? Would she be plump and happy, a small-town housewife, content with her lot?

"Each of the founding families tried to donate a window," Gina said, looking up at the richly colored image of St. Anthony of Padua. "This one's ours."

At the window's base was a brass plate, engraved in Italian with "Donated by the family of Mario A. Calvino."

Connor's eyes swept the other arched windows. At their bases were names now familiar to him—the Marchesi family, the Caniglia family, the Orsini family, the Fanelli family, the Alonzo family.

The church was peaceful, but it gave Connor an odd itchy feeling. The still air seemed alive somehow. History, like an animate being, seemed to hover restlessly in the shadows, watching him, measuring him.

For generations this had been Allegro's vital center, the place where its people prayed. It was the sanctuary where their most sacred ceremonies were held—the christenings, confirmations, weddings and funerals. The walls seemed permeated by stories of people whose lives were inextricably bound together.

"Look back here," Gina said, leading him to the back wall. "See this mural?"

Connor looked at it critically. It was a surprisingly good painting, depicting a crowd listening to the Sermon on the Mount. He wondered how such a small congregation had been able to acquire it.

"We're proud of this," she said, gazing up at it. "The town used festival money to bring the artist from Italy. He used townspeople for some of the models in the crowd. See this one?"

She pointed, smiling, at a young mother holding a child. She was beautiful, and she reminded Connor so forcibly of Gina that his muscles tensed.

"That's my great-great-grandmother." She smiled. "Earline's grandmother. Can you tell?"

He nodded, unsmiling.

"The spice recipe was hers. It's because of her you're here today. *She* brought you here. Strange, isn't it?"

Connor studied the woman's lovely face. He said nothing. Yes, he supposed this long-dead woman had brought him here. But it was her great-great-granddaughter, so like her, who kept him in Allegro.

Gina laughed, pointing to a sleepy-looking man holding the reins of a donkey. "And that's my great-great-grandfather Calvino. He said he looked so droopy because he was tired from harvest. I never knew him. But Earline has a hundred stories about him."

Connor scanned the mural, still not smiling. One figure in the background had a face like Loren's. It was hardly surprising, he thought, that he'd recognized those innocuous features; he'd certainly seen enough of them.

Gina's smile faded. She pointed at the figure. "That's Loren's great-great-grandfather, Thomaso Galli. Oh, and here's one of Wesley Dean's relatives, Marco Lorenzo."

Connor turned away. He felt an irrational edge of sick anger cut through him.

"What's wrong?" Gina asked, surprise in her voice.

"Nothing. This town really has you all trussed up, doesn't it? You're tied up to it ten thousand ways."

"I've always said so, haven't I?"

"Yes. You've always said so. Let's go."

Gina looked at him, puzzled by his mercurial change of mood. Right before they'd entered the church he'd been funny and irreverent. Now he seemed out of sorts, almost gloomy.

"You're really not tied to anywhere?" she asked, staring up at his somber profile. "Not anyplace at all?"

He seemed about to answer her, but then merely shrugged. "Let's go," he repeated.

Connor fell so silent he seemed remote, and Gina didn't understand. He hardly spoke all the way to Mott's Pond. When they reached Mott's Meadow, he shifted restlessly, as if anxious to be moving again.

She doubted that this particular excursion was a good idea. When she parked the car and got out to open the big farm gate, she said, "We have to walk the rest of the way. Are you up to it?"

"I'd walk to Cucamonga if I could," he said, taking up his crutches. If anything, he looked more bored and irritable than before. "Is this trespassing?"

"Of course not," Gina said as he made his way from the car. "The Motts are related to the Orsinis, and the Orsinis are related to everybody. I'm an Orsini on my mother's side. We just have to leave the gate as we found it. That's country etiquette."

"You're probably tempting me in so a bull will charge me," Connor muttered, frowning as he stumped past her.

Gina swung the gate shut behind them. She quickly caught up to Connor, then matched her pace to his. "The Motts don't have a bull. All we're liable to meet are frogs— and Boston Charlie."

He gave her a dubious look. "Who, I'm afraid to ask, is Boston Charlie?"

"A retired Shetland pony."

"He retired from being a pony? What is he now? An aardvark?"

"I mean, nobody rides him anymore. He's too old and creaky, and he's blind in one eye. If he tries to run, he has an asthma attack."

Connor snorted. "Sounds like a candidate for the glue factory."

Gina shook her head and thrust her hands into the pockets of her denim skirt. "Never. He's part of the family. Every year he's in the festival parade. He ends it. Somebody leads him, and he wears signs on both sides. They say, 'That's it.' He limps along, but he loves it. He's a ham."

"Cute," Connor said sarcastically.

"We like it," Gina said. "Are you sure you can navigate this road? It's rough."

"I'll do anything before I'm shut up in that house again. I'll braid ribbons into Boston Charlie's hair. I'll sit out here and make every frog a harness."

She glanced up at him. "Are you always this restless?"

"This town makes me restless. This place makes me restless. *You* make me restless."

She picked a sprig of Queen Anne's lace and twirled it between her fingers. "You really don't have a hometown?"

He frowned against the glare of the afternoon sunshine. "No."

"But you were born somewhere. Where?"

His tight smile was mocking. "Monte Carlo. My father thought they had another two weeks to gamble. He was wrong. I was almost born at the blackjack table."

His tone was sardonic, but Gina was impressed in spite of herself. Monte Carlo sounded as exotic as the moon to her. "Your parents lived in Monte Carlo?"

He shook his head. "They jetted around. Then they got divorced and fought. I'd go with one, then the other. Neither of them liked to stay in one place for long."

She looked up at him, concern on her face. "They fought over who got to take you? That's awful. I'm sorry."

He gave her his familiar crooked smile. "Not over who got to take me—over who *had* to take me. I didn't mind. I'd seen more of the world by the time I was eight than most people ever see. People like you, for instance."

"I wouldn't trade my childhood for yours," Gina answered, appalled. "Not for anything. You never settled anywhere?"

"Three years at school in England. But different schools. And not consecutive years."

"That's all?" she asked, unable to imagine such a vagabond existence.

He shook his head. "Once. My mother got married again. Every husband was a new phase. She married an older guy named Fred Mercator. They were going to spend two years plying the Caribbean on his yacht. Mercator didn't have any children, but he'd wanted to. My mother tried to foist me off on him."

He laughed. "I was ten. It almost worked, too. That yacht was a magic carpet to me. And Mercator was like a wizard, an old guy, bald, with a white beard, but a kid himself at heart. Jeez, he had a tutor on board for me and everything. It was like paradise."

Gina's brow furrowed. "What happened?"

Connor's jaw tightened. "He died. One morning he and I were raising a sail. He said, 'It's a good life, isn't it, boy?' The next thing I knew, he…just crumpled up and fell. Then he was…gone."

Gina resisted the urge to reach out and touch his arm. She resisted partly because of the expression on his face, which told her he never wanted anyone to touch him in sympathy.

He looked tall, strong, invulnerable and proud, as if he would never allow anything to hurt him again.

"What happened then?" she asked hesitantly.

His eyes went cold. "What you'd expect. My mother sold the yacht and went off to Barbados with the tutor. The sister went back to California. I got sent to school in New Hampshire. Lord, I thought winter there would last forever."

Mott's Pond appeared before them, almost hidden by the weedy screen of wildflowers. Connor frowned against the glare of the sun reflected on its surface. "Moving around became a habit. Once I stayed at college in Los Angeles for two years. My mother was dying. She decided she wanted me near. Why, I never understood."

They had reached the pond. A few wizened apple trees guarded its west side, and a stand of cattails commanded its east. Lily pads nearly blanketed its surface, and some were in bloom. On a half-sunken log, a large turtle sunned himself. When he heard their approach he slid soundlessly into the water and disappeared.

"So, this is Mott's famous pond," Connor said. "Now what?"

Suddenly Gina realized the pond must seem ridiculously insignificant to a man as worldly as Connor. Disconcerted, she kept twirling the sprig of wildflower. "At the pond you do pondy things. Fish. Catch frogs. Watch the reflection of clouds in the water. Pick flowers. Think."

"Let's just walk around it."

"You're sure you're not too tired?"

"I like to keep moving."

She nodded. *Always remember that,* she told herself. *He's warned you often enough—he likes to keep moving.*

"Did you finish college?" she asked, shielding her eyes against the brightness of the sun.

He shook his head. "No. I quit with one semester to go. My mother left me some money. I ended up in Texas. There was a local chain of sporting-goods shops going under. I could see it was bad management. So I sunk the money into them. Ended up traveling all over Texas for the next two years.

He nodded, remembering. "Sold that. Heard about a little air outfit—bush flying—up around the Yukon and the District of Mackenzie. Same thing—poorly managed. Another two years up there—a lot of flying around."

His mouth turned up in self-mockery. "Somehow Canada led to a string of travel agencies in New South Wales. Same story. Lousy management. I shaped them up and moved on. So I bought the Vagabond chain. Changed management and made myself editor-at-large. Just helled around Europe for a year, straightening out the foreign offices. And seeing if the old sights still thrilled me. They didn't."

Gina, not knowing what to say, paused by a gnarled apple tree. She reached up for an apple that was pale green, streaked with red and nearly ripe. She held it toward him.

He shook his head. "No, thanks. I might start thinking, like you, that this place is Eden."

Gina ducked her head and started walking again. She polished the apple on her skirt. "You said you wanted a boat now. Why?"

"I knew Beekman from my California days. Last year, when I was in the hospital, I heard that he'd foreclosed on a sugarcane grower in the Caribbean. Part of the settlement was a fleet of old charter yachts. One's called *The Solitaire*. That was Mercator's boat. The boat I was on when I was ten."

He glanced down at her briefly, then settled his gaze on the horizon. "The charter business sounds promising. And I'd see the Caribbean again. On *The Solitaire*. Fix her up. The world always used to look like a better place from her bridge. Maybe it will again."

Gina paused, studying him. "You're not very happy, are you? You always laugh at things and make jokes, but you're really not happy."

She saw defensive anger spark deep in his eyes. "I could say the same for you. You've got a million-dollar smile and a ninety-eight-cent life. Beekman's offering you a better chance, but you're too stubborn to listen to sense. Frankly, I don't see what you've got to smile about."

She gestured toward the meadow and pond. "I've got a wonderful life. I've been showing you—haven't you seen anything?"

He turned from her, staring off at the horizon again. "Yeah. But I see it as it is. You see it through rose-colored glasses."

He leaned on his crutch, cast her a brief scathing look over his shoulder, then turned away again. "What'll you do when you're an old woman, and Mott's Pond's been filled in, so condos can cover this meadow? And Luke Caniglia's field of flowers is plowed under for the same reason?

"What'll you do when half of Milledgeville comes flooding onto this land? And when all of a sudden your pretty little church is too little, and nobody thinks it's pretty anymore, so they tear it down and build a new one?"

"Stop it," Gina said sharply.

He swung around to face her again. "Stop it?" His smile was hard. "You might as well tell time to stop. What'll become of you, Gina? You and Earline don't have much. What happens in an emergency? What if Earline gets sick? She doesn't look good, you know. What happens when she's gone? You're going to keep that big house on the little you make? Living in an old house with your old pictures and your old memories and dead dreams?"

"*Stop it,*" she repeated.

He stepped closer. "No. You stop it. Don't let it happen. I've seen one woman waste her life that way and it wasn't a pretty sight. Beekman's willing to offer you sixty thousand dollars. Do you understand that? Sixty thousand. And I think I can finagle you a percentage. If you're careful, you and Earline could be set for life. Now you're just two women in a dying little town, and all you can depend on is luck. Luck runs out.''

''I'm lucky enough,'' Gina said with defiance. ''I'm luckier than you. At least I *have* a home—so stop harassing me. I won't listen to any more.'' Her tone changed to one of artificial cheer. ''Besides, here comes Boston Charlie.''

Connor scowled in frustration, but she ignored him. Her gaze was fixed, instead, on an ugly old pony that hobbled toward them through the weeds and wildflowers.

''I'm supposed to stop arguing because a horse is coming?'' he asked acidly.

''You're supposed to stop arguing because it's a waste of time. Hello, Charlie. Want an apple?''

The pony's arthritic gait quickened, its head bobbing with each step. The once golden coat was grizzled and slightly moth-eaten, showing more than one bare patch. A thick white forelock nearly covered its eyes, one of which was squinted shut.

''Charlie,'' Gina almost cooed, ''bonny baby Boston Charlie. Want an apple, sweetie? It's fresh off the tree.''

Connor made a sound of disgust. ''I've seen dead horses in better shape. That's not a real pony. It's a zombie.''

Gina broke off a piece of apple and fed it to Boston Charlie. He drooled as he chewed, but Gina hugged his neck, pressing her face against his mane. ''He's a darling, and everybody loves him.'' She gave Connor a dismissive glance. ''You don't have a real heart. You've got a zombie heart.''

''He drools. He's got bald spots.''

''So? Maybe you will, too, someday. Does that mean nobody should love you?''

Connor turned away, shaking his head. ''Doesn't sixty thousand dollars mean anything to you, Gina? Or are you so naive you can't even imagine it? Is that it? Have you been listening to me?''

She refused to listen to him, and she refused to answer. She gave Boston Charlie another bite of apple and hugged him more tightly than before. "Izzy cute-ums pony? Izzy-wizzy cutest 'ittle pony in the whole big world? Izzy Gina's 'ittle darling pony-boy?''

"Take me back," Connor muttered. "I'd rather be in solitary confinement than hear this slop.''

Gina straightened, but kept scratching Charlie behind the ears. "You won't be in solitary confinement. Wesley's coming over to sit with you.''

"No, he's not. He's not a child. He's some sort of evil space alien. Keep him away from me.''

Gina stepped to his side and narrowed her eyes. "You really *are* a zombie. Wesley's an unhappy little boy who doesn't fit in and whose father's sick. You said once you knew how it felt to be different. But you don't. You pretend. Maybe you're just dead inside, completely dead. You couldn't be nice to Wesley if you tried.''

His eyebrow arched dangerously. Then, slowly, he smiled. "You're a strange one to make accusations.''

She clenched her fists. "Why?''

"You, trying to keep your heart in a grave when it's not dead. Your narrow little life, bounded on one side by Mott's Pond and on the other by an old man's garden. Do you really think you're more alive than I am? Maybe I could teach you a thing or two about living.''

"And maybe I could teach *you* a few things. Did you ever think of that?'' She squared her shoulders and brushed her wind-tossed hair back from her face.

Connor studied her full lips with an interest so frank it was insolent. "Yes," he said. "I've thought of that. I thought of it all night long.''

Gina's patience, strained too far, snapped. "I told you— I won't listen to that kind of talk!'' She started back toward the car, intending to set off at her swiftest pace, letting him follow as best he could.

She was astonished when his hand shot out, his fingers closing around her upper arm.

She wheeled to face him. "Don't touch me."

His eyes were blue fire, and the hair that blew across his brow shimmered in the hot sunlight. "Why? Afraid you'll like it? You do like it, you know."

Gina found it hard to breathe. She glared at him, her heart thudding painfully.

"What's the matter?" he asked, bending nearer, making her pulses drum harder. "Afraid you'll end up in my arms again?"

She stared up at him, wondering if it was about to happen again—that he would commandeer her lips as boldly as a pirate, and she, overwhelmed, would not resist him.

He drew her nearer, leaning so that his eyes were level with hers. "What's the matter?" he asked with dangerous softness. "You're trembling. You want to believe it's from fear or anger. But it's not. You know what it is, and so do I. I'm not the one who scares or angers you. It's you. It's your own desire."

"Stop flattering yourself." Her voice was uneven.

His hand tightened. "I'm not. Stop lying to yourself."

"I'm not."

"I could kiss you now. You'd let me. But then you'd run away. Like always."

"No."

His lips drew nearer. "Don't worry," he said with the same alarming quiet. "I'm tired of trying to save you. You want kisses, Gina. In fact, you want far more than kisses. But I won't try to convince you. The next time I touch you, it'll be because you ask."

"Never," Gina said with passion. But she stood as if hypnotized, unable to break away.

He smiled. "Never's a long time."

He lowered his face so that his mouth nearly brushed hers, and Gina, dazed by conflicting emotions, let her eyes flutter shut. She felt the warmth of his breath on her moist lips and trembled harder.

But he didn't kiss her. Instead, his hand dropped away, releasing her. She stared up at him, disconcerted.

"You're ready for worlds beyond Mott's Pond. You're ready for men beyond Loren."

He shook his head. Something haunted, almost sad, played in his smile. "I may be the first, but I shouldn't be the last. I'm just here to open the door for you. To show what's possible. So much is. In your heart you know it."

She blinked in confusion. The sky behind him blazed too hotly, gilded his hair too brightly. Somewhere in the lacy weeds, a meadowlark began to carol, and Gina felt, oddly, as if her heart were rising heavenward with each note. It left an empty ache in her chest.

"Between you and me," she said, her voice tight, "there can't ever be anything. Nothing's possible."

The lark sang more raptly. Connor's mouth kept its troubled line. "I told you, I'm only here to open doors. Isn't that enough?"

She turned her face away and tried to lose herself in the exultation of the lark's song, the beauty of the day.

"We'll see," Connor said cryptically.

She sensed his eyes on her, and she straightened her backbone to make it stop tingling. She bit her lower lip. She knew he was right. If he tried to kiss her, she would let him. But she could not ask him to do so. She could not.

"I'll make a bargain with you," he said. "For the next week, show me this town as you see it. If you can convince me you're right about it—and about yourself—I'll leave you in peace. I'll tell Beekman to do the same, that you can't be moved. And you can stay here, true to your dying town and ghostly lover."

He paused. She tried to show no reaction because she sensed him closely watching for one.

When he spoke again, his voice was the peculiar half growl, half purr that made her skin prickle. "Fair enough?"

He'll leave, she thought, *and then I'll be safe again.* She turned and gave him a brittle little smile. She nodded.

"Fair enough," she said. But she didn't dare to meet his eyes.

CHAPTER ELEVEN

OVER THE NEXT FEW DAYS Gina and Connor developed an uneasy routine. In the mornings, after Earline left, Gina drove him around Allegro and the surrounding farmland.

She struggled to tell him, as unemotionally as possible, the history, legends and lore of the town. But try as she might, she never sounded neutral about the place she loved so well. Often she found his gaze resting on her, half mocking, half puzzled.

On Thursday morning, the day before the festival began, she took him to another meadow. They sat at its edge, watching the wildflowers nod in the breeze. Gina told Connor that once a fine house had stood there. Years ago it had been the scene of a wonderful party, the most elaborate ever held in Allegro.

Gina's grandmother, only sixteen then, had been invited to attend by the most handsome young man in town. For such a special occasion, she'd been given her first store-bought dress. She'd baked a beautiful cake, as well, so she could ask the young man in for refreshments after the party.

Gina laughed ruefully as she watched a butterfly dancing among the larkspur. "But," she said, "when they came back to her house, she opened the door and there was the hound dog, standing in the middle of the kitchen table, eating the cake. She was humiliated."

Gina shook her head. "But there was worse. Later she found she'd worn her new dress backward—that's how little she knew about store-bought clothes. And some of the girls at the party had laughed behind her back. She felt terrible."

Connor watched her dimples play. "And the beau?"

Gina shrugged, picked several long-stemmed clover blossoms and began weaving them into a chain. "He heard that she cried. So he came and told her she was prettier with her dress on wrong than any girl he'd ever seen with her dress on right. I don't know what he said about the dog and the cake. But it must have been the right thing. They got married."

Connor made no reply for a moment, only watched her braid her chain of clover. At last he asked, "Did she have dimples like yours, your grandmother?"

Gina smiled at the question. "Yes. Why?"

"Nothing," Connor muttered. "I thought so, that's all." He forced himself to stop looking at her. He picked a sprig of clover and cast it away, frowning.

ALMOST AGAINST HIS WILL, Connor began to understand. There was no corner of Allegro that didn't hold memories for Gina. It seemed that as a child, she had played hopscotch on every sidewalk, climbed every tree, visited every house, known every family down to their dogs, cats, parakeets and hamsters.

She showed him the big oleander bush beneath which her cousin Lucia had hidden the day she tried to run away from home. She pointed out the venerable oak tree in the park that Earline had fallen out of as a child. Both Earline and the oak had been small then. She showed him where the drugstore had once stood, recounted how she and her friends used to drink sodas there after school and told him how Snicky Alonzo used to sit outside the store on weekends, showing the children how to do yo-yo tricks.

He saw the town's dusty baseball field, where Gina's father had once hit the winning run against Allegro's archrival, Milledgeville. He hobbled beside her through the field beyond the parish hall, where, for decades, the carnival had set up.

Gina pointed out the place where, as a child, she had fallen off the merry-go-round. She showed him precisely where the Ferris wheel always stood. Years ago John Orsini had proposed to Mary Ellen there, while their car swung back and forth, poised at the wheel's highest point. Poor Mary Ellen had been too motion sick to answer.

Gina showed him the exact spot where the popcorn booth always was and told how last year someone had thrown a rubber frog into the popper and how Billy Ray Fenelli had split his Elvis pants.

She seemed acquainted with every pebble, every blade of grass, every clover blossom and dust mote in Allegro.

He teased her by telling of his escapades in Paris, Milan, Dublin, London, Frankfurt, Barcelona, Los Angeles, Boston, Melbourne, Fairbanks, Cancun. She always smiled, fascinated, but to Connor's disgruntlement, she also looked as if she was perfectly happy where she was.

His afternoons were less intriguing. Gina went running off to do a dozen things, to mind her shop, help at the parish hall or tend to festival business. Connor wished she wouldn't go, but if she had to, he wished she'd at least let him brood alone and in peace. He found himself brooding a good deal lately.

But instead of the consolation of solitude, he had to endure the company of Wesley Dean. Perversely Connor took to sunning himself in the backyard, hoping the heat would drive Wesley back into his air-conditioned house. But Wesley was made of sterner stuff. He perspired until his glasses slipped down his nose, but he wanted his dollar an hour. He stayed.

The afternoon before the festival began, Connor sat shirtless in a lawn chair, his foot propped up on a stool. The scent of the spice field reminded him, as always, of Gina, and made him restless.

He played a tedious card game with Wesley. The game, called Sheep Head, had such complicated rules that Connor darkly suspected Wesley had made them up.

"You can't take that," Connor protested when Wesley began to rake in the cards to count his points.

"Can so," Wesley said smugly. "The jack is higher than the ace."

"Yeah, yeah, yeah, and clubs beat spades. None of this makes sense."

"It does if you're a good card player." Wesley smirked, then looked thoughtful. "Did you really almost get your foot cut off by a motorboat? In Spain? In the ocean?"

"Yes. There was lots of blood. You would have loved it."

"Have you been in oceans much? Have you ever been bit by a shark?" Wesley asked, interest piqued.

"As a matter of a fact, I have."

"Wow! and you lived to tell?"

"It was a small shark. Only fifty pounds or so." He showed Wesley the scar, long since healed, just under his elbow.

"Wow! What'd you do?"

Connor, who wasn't used to children, was surprised at Wesley's enthusiasm. "I punched him in the nose. Sharks have tender snouts. If one comes for you, punch his nose."

"Wow!" Wesley repeated raptly. "Have you ever been bit by a piranha fish?"

Connor grinned crookedly, remembering Fred Mercator. "No. But I had a stepfather who was. Scars all over one hand."

"Tell me, will you, huh? Huh?"

Anything was better than playing Sheep Head, so Connor talked about Fred Mercator's adventures. The old man had once kept Connor amused for hours with his tales, and now Connor spun them out for Wesley.

By late afternoon, Connor was unsettled by the realization that Wesley had started to *like* him. The boy was, in fact, looking at him with a trace of hero worship.

"You know," Wesley said, abashed, "I kind of hated you when you first showed up. You took Gina away."

"I'll be gone soon," Connor answered dryly. "You'll have her back."

Wesley pulled up his T-shirt and scratched a mosquito bite on his round stomach. "Well, see, I was gonna marry her when I grow up." He studied the mosquito bite with scientific interest and scratched harder. "It's okay, though," he said. "You can have her."

"Have her? Marry her?" Connor asked blankly.

Wesley pulled down his shirt and gave his stomach one last scratch through the fabric. "Yeah. See, she's going to be kind of old. I can't marry her for about twenty years. So maybe she should marry somebody already old. Like you."

Chagrined, Connor crooked an eyebrow. "I see."

Wesley's face went solemn. "My dad's real old," he said. "He's forty-nine. He had a heart attack. He's supposed to come home from the hospital in two days. A heart attack doesn't always kill you, does it?"

Connor glanced away, embarrassed because he thought he saw fear, real and naked, in the child's eyes.

He remembered Fred Mercator saying, "It's a good life, isn't it, boy?" before falling down with a heart attack, dead almost instantly.

"Naw," he said gruffly. "It doesn't have to kill you. Don't worry, okay?"

Wesley was silent a moment. When he spoke again, his voice was hesitant. "Did you ever know anybody that died of a heart attack?"

Connor found himself lying. "No," he said shortly. "Nobody."

But once more the image of Fred Mercator's death flashed through his mind. He supposed, cynically, that his childhood had died at the same moment Mercator's heart stopped beating.

"Hey, guys..." Gina's voice interrupted his moody reverie. She stood on the back porch, wearing cutoffs, a bright pink top, a pink baseball cap, and her wide smile with both dimples showing. "Why so glum?" she asked. "Festival starts tomorrow."

He found, suddenly, that he was smiling and that Wesley was, too.

As Connor gazed at her, something inside his chest wrenched. *Damn,* he thought, as it twisted harder and more inexplicably. *What's wrong with me? I've got to get out of this town. Soon.*

In the back of his mind he'd been putting together a plan that would satisfy everybody, Gina, Beekman, even himself. Then he'd be on his way to the Caribbean, back on Mercator's yacht once more. He'd leave the woman taken care of, but far behind. He'd be free again.

THAT EVENING, Connor asked Gina to take him for a drive in the MG. She chauffeured him past the parish grounds and the neighboring fields. The carnival people had arrived that afternoon. Magically, rides and game booths now sprawled across land that had been empty only the day before.

The unlit Ferris wheel, dark against the twilight sky, loomed above all else, taller than any building or tree in Allegro. Workers scurried around, checking equipment, nailing up signs, erecting still more booths.

Connor stared at them suspiciously. "How many people come to town with this outfit?"

"About two hundred," she answered, smiling at the sight of the Ferris wheel. "They have trailers. They camp in one of Donny Orsini's fields."

"They're rough, carnival people," he said, frowning. "Isn't there trouble when they come?"

Gina shook her head. "This is a good company, good people. They run it straight. We're very careful about that. And we always hire about thirty deputies to take care of the traffic and make sure there's no trouble."

He watched how high she held her head, how her auburn curls streamed in the wind. "So you think you've got it down to a science?"

She gave him a teasing look. "Oh, I forgot. You're Mr. Miracle Manager. You'd do it better. What would you change?"

He didn't smile. "Plenty, if I had to. It's just another management job. But it's not mine. Mine is to be the go-between for you and Beekman."

Her dimples disappeared and the line of her mouth straightened. "I have nothing to say to Beekman."

He raked his fingers impatiently through his hair. "Look, I've been thinking about this mess. I've got some ideas. Let's park someplace and talk."

"We've talked all week. I have to help Earline pack elephants. She's working too hard. She's worn out."

"That's one of the things I want to talk about—Earline. You don't admit it, but you worry about her."

Gina shrugged. "I worry about everybody I love. Don't you?"

"I don't love anybody, and I don't intend to. Listen, park. Let's talk. Maybe I can solve this problem."

She kept her face blank. "I don't have any problem. Beekman has a problem. He's not getting my recipe. No matter what he does."

Connor shifted his shoulders restlessly. "What if—" he paused "—what if I told you that if you played your cards right, you could sell the recipe, keep the festival and give this town a new lease on life? Everybody's happy—you, Beekman, the whole town."

She frowned in puzzled disbelief. "What are you up to now? What do you do all afternoon—just sit and scheme?"

"I was born to scheme. I do it better than anybody I know. Are you going to listen or not?"

They were driving through the deserted downtown. Gina slowed the MG and pulled to a stop in front of her antique shop, Remembrance.

Connor eyed the place critically. Its wooden facade badly needed paint, and its big glass window, cracked across the top, was patched with tape. The finest treasures of Gina's store were ranged in the window display: a spinning wheel, a wooden butter churn, a brass postal scale, a set of rose-patterned dishes. Next to the dishes sat an antique doll dressed in yellowing lace.

To Connor they seemed dubious treasures, paltry. How long could she make a living from such a small store so far off the beaten track? One good-size emergency could wipe her out. Then, if Beekman still wanted the recipe, she'd be at his mercy. She'd have to take whatever she could get.

He pressed his fist against the dashboard and leaned toward her intently. An almost ferocious seriousness shone in his eyes. "Don't interrupt me. Don't say anything till I'm finished. Understand?"

Taken aback, Gina nodded. She had gone to great pains to keep Connor at an emotional distance, and she had forced herself to think of him not as a man but an opponent, one she must be polite to but wary of. It was suddenly impossible to forget he was a man—and a dangerously arresting one.

"You love this town. You love your festival. But your town's drying up because there's no industry. *Bring* industry here. Tell Beekman you'll sell the recipe—ask for forty thousand, not the sixty he's prepared to pay. That'll soften the blow."

Gina shook her head in perplexity. "What blow?"

Connor bent closer. "Don't say anything, not yet. Just listen. Tell Beekman you'll sell the recipe—but only if he manufactures the sauce here. He buys the cannery, reopens it, creates a new job market.''

Her mouth parted in surprise. ''But—''

He laid his finger against her lips. She was chagrined that even so slight a touch shuddered through her veins, burning like fire.

''Shh,'' he warned. ''That's your first condition. He reopens the cannery. The tomato farmers have their market back. The farms stay profitable. Nobody has to sell out—not yet, anyway.

''The second condition is this—the town keeps the festival. You retain the use of the recipe for that one charitable purpose, no other. You never *sell* the spices again. But you keep the tradition just as it was.''

He took his finger from her lips, leaned his fist against the dashboard again. His eyes, with their almost hypnotic energy, held hers. ''It won't save this town forever,'' he said, his voice low. ''Nothing can. But it can help it survive...who knows how long? Maybe for your lifetime, at least. Think of it, Gina. The town goes on, your whole life long. Is that good enough for you?''

His proposition was so unexpected, so bold, so impossible, it stunned her. Trade the recipe so that Allegro would once more have industry and jobs? Would Beekman even agree to such a wild proposal? If he would, how could she resist? She leaned against the door, feeling almost faint.

''He'd never...it wouldn't,'' she stammered. ''I can't...I promised my father—''

Once more Connor laid his finger against her lips. ''Your father would have traded the recipe if it meant the good of his neighbors, the good of the town. Even your precious saintly Loren would have. And they'd want you to, wouldn't they? Deny it. You can't.''

Confused, stunned, she tried to turn her face away, but he caught her chin between his thumb and forefinger, forcing her to meet his eyes. ''It's the perfect answer, Gina. It's the only one. We all get what we want—you, me, Beekman. If he agrees, you can't say no. You know it, and I know it."

"I—I—" Gina stuttered. Tears sprang to her eyes. "What if he won't agree?"

"He has to. It's the only way he gets the recipe." His voice softened. "Don't cry, Gina. It's the right thing. And when it's done, I'll be gone. I won't be here to make you cry anymore."

"You—you—" She struggled to get her breath. "It's not you. I mean, I'm happy, I really am. I mean, it might work. You're almost like a genius, Connor. But then, if you fix everything, you'll...you'll go away?"

His touch grew gentler as his hand framed her jaw. He nodded. His blond forelock almost touched her bangs. "I go away. Like I always said. But if you wanted me to—" his voice grew softer "—I could kiss you goodbye. Maybe even kiss away those tears. But only if you asked."

The tears in her eyes grew larger until finally one spilled down her cheek. It sparkled in the light of the rising moon. *Kiss my tears away,* she wanted to say. *Oh, please, Connor, hold me tight and kiss them away. You're the only one who can. But don't go. Please don't go.*

Conflicting emotions crossed his face. She knew he wanted to kiss her as badly as she wanted his kiss. But she could see from the stubborn set of his mouth, the tautness of his jaw, that he meant what he said. He was leaving and he would not be back.

He would try to give her what she wanted most. But then he would go because, like the wind, he could not be tied to one place. Free, he would disappear forever, more of a phantom than even Loren had become. If he kissed her now, he would burn the memory of himself into her heart so deeply she knew she could not bear it.

"I can't ask that," she said, brushing the tear away. "Not now. When you really go, maybe. But not now. I just can't...."

He bent a fraction of an inch nearer, as if he would kiss her anyway. He tipped her face up imperceptibly closer to his.

"No," she breathed again. "Don't."

His eyes held hers for a moment. Then his hand fell from her face and he turned away. He laughed, a short harsh sound. "Let's go home. You wrap elephants, and I'll call Beekman. And we'll end this farce."

GINA WENT STRAIGHT to her room, trying to gather her thoughts. She stood in its center, clenching and unclenching her fists. Strewn across the dresser top were her souvenirs and photos of Loren.

The bulletin board, covered with snapshots of the two of them, leaned against the wall. The bear he had given her so long ago lay on its back on her pillow, its black eyes staring at nothing, its tattered arms embracing nothing.

In the car with Connor, she had just done what she'd sworn she'd never do. She'd agreed to sell the recipe—if Beekman met her terms. Would he? She had no idea and she could not sort out her feelings. Would she be glad if he agreed? Or relieved if he did not? She truly didn't know. The whole idea seemed too unlikely, almost fantastical. It numbed her.

She stepped to the dresser and picked up Loren's college portrait. Connor had been right—Loren would have said to sell the recipe if it meant saving the town. Her father would have said so, too. She knew it.

She studied Loren's picture, trying to soothe herself with his familiar features. But for the first time, his face did not seem as familiar as it once had. The numbness that gripped her grew deeper.

Loren had been twenty-two when the photo was taken. She had been barely twenty. Now she was four years older than he had been. She realized, without emotion, that the passing years had made his haircut seem a bit quaint and his unlined face boyish.

He *was* boyish, she thought; he always had been, and he always would be. He was frozen away from time, outside its stream, but it was carrying her onward, farther and farther from him. She had loved this boy, and in memory she would always love him, although she could never reach out to him again.

Now another man's lips had touched hers, another man's arms had held her, and she feared, unhappily, that she might be in love with him. He was not the sort to return her love. He was not the sort at all.

She set down Loren's photo and picked up a smaller framed snapshot of the two of them at Loren's house, at his birthday party. She'd been fifteen then; he, eighteen.

The two people in the picture looked impossibly young and innocent. She shook her head.

"You'd never have believed how complicated life gets," she whispered to them sadly.

Then she opened the top drawer and began to put the pictures and souvenirs away. Connor would be going away soon, but he had accomplished what he'd intended. He'd changed her forever. She did not even know if the change was for good or bad, only that it could not be undone.

CONNOR GRITTED HIS TEETH and hated life. He was accomplishing nothing he'd set out to do. Nothing. Not one damned thing.

He had shut himself in the kitchen and had been arguing long-distance with Beekman for half an hour.

Beekman's voice came over the phone like the icy buzz of some angry insect. "I won't be blackmailed," he said. "I won't be railroaded. I'm offering her money and that's all I'm offering her, by hell and by horseradish."

"Then you won't get the recipe, Morty," Connor said. "The woman's only got one weakness, and it's this town. There's no other way to get what you want."

"I will not," Beekman vowed, "buy some termite-ridden cannery in Arkansas when I have excellent canneries in Monterey. Why should I pay farmers in Arkansas to grow tomatoes, when I own the biggest—and best—damn tomato farm in California? I'm in the business of making money, not stuffing it down a rat hole."

"Look," Connor muttered, "think of it as expanding your empire. The cannery here is feasible—"

"In a pig's eye it's feasible! They can't even grow enough tomatoes to keep it open year-round. I'd have to truck them up from Texas. I have a king's ransom in tomatoes *here*. I have state-of-the-art canneries *here*. I will not kowtow to some silly sentiment."

"What about the festival?" Connor persisted. "You were willing to have that here."

"Because it's already established. But a pox on her if she won't cooperate. I'll have my own festival in Milledgeville and drive Allegro out of business. Ladies who make spaghetti I can always hire. Allegro—it's dying. Who needs it?"

"I thought you had vision, Morty."

"You give me visions of ruin and bankruptcy. I'll have that recipe with no conditions whatsoever. I'll have it for cash and cash alone. If you can't get it for me, I'll find someone who can. And in the meantime, you can kiss *The Solitaire* and all the yachts goodbye. I'll keep them myself, you loser."

"You're the loser, Beekman," Connor snarled. "This is an opportunity. It's an excellent location, far more central than Monterey. It's got tax incentives, lower labor, lower overhead—"

"Then buy it yourself," Beekman retorted. "I want a recipe, not a rehab program for some town tottering at death's door."

"It's the only way you'll get the recipe. Do I have to spell it out for you?"

"There's more than one way to skin a cat. Someday, sooner or later, something will happen. She'll need money. Then she'll come crawling, and I'll make the terms, not her. As for *The Solitaire,* I'll make her into a floating restaurant for fat-cat tourists. Eat your heart out, Munroe."

"You wanted a deal with Calvino. I've got you a deal."

"Bah!" exclaimed Beekman. "I spit on such a deal. Don't waste my time."

GINA STOOD in the dining room, wrapping the last elephant in tissue paper. When Connor pushed open the door, she took one look at his face and knew. She dropped her gaze to the elephant again and pretended to adjust its wrap.

"He said no, didn't he?" she asked, her head down.

Connor, with the aid of of his crutches, hobbled to the other side of the table. He shrugged. "For now he says no. Minds change."

The silence lay heavy between them.

"Maybe it's for the best," she said at last. "Who can say?"

He had no answer. For a few giddy hours, he had seen himself a hero, *her* hero. Now he saw himself for what he was—a man powerless to change the slightest thing in her life. It was a good thing he would soon be gone. He wasn't used to failure and he didn't like it. It made him think of Fanny Mercator again.

"Where's Earline?" he asked, to break the unhappy silence.

"She went to bed. She wasn't feeling well. She complained she had pains in her chest."

Connor looked up sharply, but still she kept her face averted, and he couldn't read her expression. "Pains in her chest?" He thought of Mercator's heart attack and of Wesley's father. He wondered if Gina knew chest pains could be a serious warning sign.

"She says it's nothing," Gina said, laying the elephant in a cardboard carton. "She says it's only heartburn."

"Gina?"

"Yes?" She looked up and seemed to flinch slightly as she met his eyes.

"Are you happy about Beekman—or sad?"

She gave a wan smile. "I don't really know. I would have felt funny about selling it. I did promise my father it'd always stay in the family."

"And you don't take promises lightly. You couldn't if you tried. But listen, he may come through yet. He's an eccentric old coot, Beekman."

She shook her head doubtfully. "No. Nobody would buy that cannery. Or invest in Allegro. I guess I knew it—in my heart."

He tried again. "You don't know. He may think things over and change his mind."

"No." She paused and gave Connor a searching look. "I'm sorry...about your boat. I know it means a lot to you."

He shrugged. "A boat's a boat."

"But it was his boat—Mercator's," she said. "You were happy on it. Will you...will you still go to the Caribbean?"

He glanced about the room. It seemed ominously empty with all the elephants packed away. He shrugged again. "I can be happy anywhere. I heard about some mills in Korea that might be for sale. It calls for heavy investment, but there's good money to be made in Korea. It's a country with potential."

"It's a long way off," she said. "But that's what you love best, isn't it?"

He stared at her for several seconds, trying to choose his answer. He'd promised himself not to lie to her again, and he didn't intend to. He took a deep breath and cursed the tang of the spice field that always hung in the summer air. "Yes," he said. "It's what I love best. Always have. Always will."

She was silent, watching him.

"Gina," he said softly, "I can't stay anywhere for long. It's not in me. Korea's as good as the Caribbean and Timbuktu's as good as either. As long is it's someplace new. That's all that counts for me. It's all that ever has."

She smiled as if she understood. Then they both looked away. There was nothing more to say.

CHAPTER TWELVE

THE NEXT MORNING Earline still did not feel well. When she tried to rise, she was weak and dizzy, and the pains in her chest had returned. Gina made her stay in bed.

Distracted, she literally flew around the kitchen, trying to do a dozen things at once. Connor, seated at the kitchen table, frowned as he watched. She was trying to make both coffee and tea, toast bread, cook oatmeal, poach eggs and squeeze orange juice. She had stacked the boxes of elephants next to the kitchen door, and they towered there, waiting to be loaded into the car.

She kept trying to phone the medical center in Milledgeville, but it was too early. The switchboard wasn't open.

Connor rose and stumped to the counter on his crutches. "Here," he muttered, taking the orange from her hand. "Let me. You can't do everything. And I'll watch the eggs. You tend to Earline."

Gina ran her hand through her bangs worriedly. "I should have known. Every year she works herself into a state over the festival, and now she's actually made herself sick. If I can't get somebody to take over her booth, she'll get even worse. But I can't—I have to take her to a doctor. And who'll take *my* place? I'm supposed to be heading the salad crew.... Oh, Earline's right, this is madness. Why do we do it?"

"Calm down," he said out of the side of his mouth. "I'll take over the elephant booth. Forget salad—Earline's more important than a bunch of lettuce."

She looked at him with gratitude. "You'll sell elephants? Oh, Connor, that'd be a lifesaver. But... do you think you can do it?"

He laughed. "I've peddled baseballs in Texas and plane rides in Alaska. What's hard about a few measly elephants?"

"Nothing," she said, but her own smile was strained. "I imagine you could do anything you set your mind to. I'll load the car. Then as soon as I can get an appointment for Earline, I'll drive you to the fairgrounds."

Gina snatched the toast from the toaster when it popped, spread it with margarine and made up a tray of toast, juice, oatmeal and herbal tea for Earline. She picked it up and bustled off to the back bedroom.

Connor looked after her, his brow creased. She seemed so damned vulnerable. Both women did, at this juncture. He put the orange in the squeezer and brought pressure down on it, wishing it were Beekman's stubborn skull he had at his mercy.

If anything was seriously wrong with Earline and Beekman found out, Connor knew that Gina would be helpless. If it was a choice between selling the recipe and Earline's health, she wouldn't hesitate for a moment; the recipe would be Beekman's.

Damn, he thought, if Earline really was ill, it would put a whole new spin on things. Then it would practically become his *duty* to convince Gina to sell immediately, for as high a price as she could get.

And, in consequence, he might just get *The Solitaire*. It was odd how that thought gave him little pleasure.

When Gina returned, she tried to smile at Connor, but worry shadowed her eyes.

"Sit," he said. "Eat. At least have a glass of juice."

She shook her head. "No. I'll load the car, then try making some more calls."

He swung around on his crutches so that his body stood between her and the door. "I'll load the car. Sit down."

"You can't," she argued, glancing significantly at his crutches. "I won't have you take a chance on falling. I can't take care of two of you. Not while festival's on. I just can't. Don't make me worry about you, too."

He swore softly, but let her pass. "Listen," he said, watching her struggle with a box, "I'm not giving up on Beekman yet. I've got a cellular phone in my trunk. I'll take it with me, put in some calls."

She acted as if she didn't hear.

"Gina," he said, his voice harsher than he intended, "are you listening? I'm still going to try to come up with a deal you can live with. One that'll take care of all your worries. Yours and Earline's, too."

She turned and looked sadly at him over the top of the carton. "Don't you understand? I can't think of *deals* at a time like this."

His eyes flashed. "You can't afford not to."

She only shook her head. "Oh, Connor," she said with an unhappy sigh. "You really don't understand, do you?"

Somehow she managed to open the door, cart the big box through it and kick the door shut behind her.

Connor stood looking after her, gripping the crutches so hard his knuckles whitened. No, he thought, glaring at the closed door. *She* didn't understand. But he'd make her. He'd make her yet.

GINA ARRANGED a nine-thirty appointment for Earline, drove Connor to the fairgrounds and left him there, stone faced, to unpack elephants in the booth. She didn't reappear until well after one, when the craft fair and carnival had already drawn a sizable crowd. She looked tense, distraught and weary.

Connor cut short the phone call he was making, rose and drew her into the booth. "Sit," he said, nodding at the chair he'd vacated. "How's Earline?"

She sank into the chair and massaged her temples with her fingertips. She looked as if she might cry. "The doctor thinks it's angina. He's keeping her in the hospital for tests. She's upset." Gina shook her head in bewilderment. "Why am I sitting here? I need to get to the parish hall and help with the salads. I need to do a hundred things...."

She started to rise, but Connor put his hand on her shoulder. "Stay put," he ordered. "Somebody's sister-in-law's filling in for you—from Little Rock. She says she loves it, it's like old times. Come on. I'll shut up this booth. Let's get you something to eat. If I know you, you're running on empty, as usual."

"But we can't," Gina protested. "Not with all these elephants—" She stopped and stared about the booth, her lips parted in surprise. The shelves were completely empty.

"Where are the elephants?" she asked, wide-eyed. "Didn't you unpack them? Goodness, Connor, nobody'll buy them if they can't see them—"

"They've been seen. They've been bought. That's one thing you can tell Earline not to worry about."

"They're *all* sold?" Gina asked, incredulous. "But how...?"

Connor's slanted smile was smug. "Bright and early a guy from out of state came by. He deals in toys, was looking for unusual items. He loved them—bought the whole lot."

He handed her the cigar box that Earline used for a cash box and flipped it open. Gina stared down at a thick stack of fifty-dollar bills. "Seventeen hundred and fifty dollars," he said with satisfaction.

Gina couldn't help herself. Setting the box aside, she leapt to her feet and hugged him. "Oh, Connor, you're wonderful. She'll be so happy. She does worry about money."

His strong arms wound around her. "Be careful, Gina. A man could learn to like this."

"Oh," she said in embarrassment, trying to draw back. But he kept her in his embrace and smiled down sardonically.

"Don't," she said in quiet panic. "People will see."

"They already have," he murmured. "They don't seem to mind."

Gina glanced about in mortification. She realized more than one set of eyes was on them—some watching furtively, some with blatant interest. She saw Ralph Marchesi passing by. At first he looked surprised. Then, slowly, he smiled and nodded in approval.

Once more she tried to squirm away. Once more Connor held her fast. "Nice fellow, Ralph Marchesi," he said. "We talked. He introduced me to his aunt. She's got a booth of quilts. Interesting woman. She gave me a recipe for homemade spumoni."

Gina blinked with astonishment. "Sophia Marchesi gave *you* her spumoni recipe? You must have switched your charm on full force."

"A man peddling elephants can't be uppity. I tried to fit in, that's all."

"Let go, please. You embarrass me—really."

"Why be embarrassed? Because people see that a man finds you attractive?"

"Don't tease," she said fervently, staring up at him. "It's been too hard a day. Please, Connor."

His smile faded, but still he gripped her. "Promise you'll let me buy you something to eat. Then I'll let go."

His tone was playful, but the look deep in his eyes was both serious and implacable. And somehow, his touch, dangerous as it was, felt comforting. "All right. I promise. Now let go."

Slowly and with seeming reluctance, he released her.

THAT NIGHT when she got home from visiting Earline, Gina was bone weary. Connor was in the kitchen, and he had supper waiting for her. He'd brought spaghetti, garlic bread and salad from the festival. He'd kept the spaghetti hot, the bread warm, the salad cool and had a bottle of wine uncorked.

Gina smiled in disbelief as she settled into her chair. "That looks like Snicky Alonzo's homemade wine."

"It is," Connor said. He sat down across from her and poured her a glass. "It was a gift."

"He gave it to you?" Gina shook her head. "You're Mr. Popularity today. Snicky only gives his wine to people he really likes."

"He asked about Earline, and he sent this for you. You're the one he likes. Most people here seem to like you." He clicked his glass against hers. "To Earline's health. And yours."

Her face troubled, she took a sip of the strong red wine. "Earline feels better," she said. "But the doctor wants to do something called a radionuclide scan. He's certain it's angina. He wants to see how serious it is."

"Cheer up, Gina," Connor said. "Angina's no joke, but it can be treated. It doesn't necessarily mean permanent damage. It can even be a blessing in disguise—a warning to get help before something worse happens."

Gina nodded and toyed with her salad. "I know. But she needs to be under less stress. Earline's always been tense. I shouldn't let her go through all this uproar for the festival. And she's always worried about money, especially since she lost her job."

She raised her eyes to meet his. "Did you talk to Beekman again?" she asked hesitantly.

Connor's look became shuttered. "I couldn't get through to him. His secretary says he's out of the country. Maybe he is, maybe he isn't. I'm sorry, Gina."

She set down her fork. "But what's that mean? He isn't interested in the recipe anymore?"

"It means he doesn't like the way I've handled it. He doesn't want to deal with me. But he's still interested, if I know Beekman. For now he's playing hard to get. Like I said, I'm sorry."

She put her elbow on the table, closed her eyes and leaned her forehead against her hand. "I've searched my soul all day. I don't know what to think. All those things you said about the recipe, they're starting to make sense. Do you really believe them, Connor? What do you think I should do? Stop fighting? Just let Beekman have it?"

He paused. When he spoke, his voice was cavalier. "What do I think? Ask in a few days, Gina. Right now, you should drink Snicky's wine and eat Allegro's spaghetti. It's good stuff. Beekman's right about that, at least. It's wonderful. Really wonderful."

She opened her eyes, letting her hand fall back to the table. She managed a tired smile. "What? For once, you're not going to tell me what to do?"

He didn't smile in return. "I used to think I had all the answers. Not tonight."

She stared at the table, putting her hand to her forehead again. "Maybe I should call him. Maybe he'd talk to me."

"No. Wait a few days."

She nodded, closing her eyes. "You're right. I should take my time. A decision made too fast won't be a good one."

He didn't answer.

"I'm so glad Earline feels better," she said. "So glad. Thanks for helping. She was thrilled about the elephants. She thinks you're a true hero."

Again he said nothing.

She kept her eyes closed because it seemed easier to talk to him that way. "When you go, she'll miss you. I don't suppose you'll ever come back again . . . or will you?"

She heard him exhale sharply. "It's never been my style. I try not to get attached to things."

She forced herself to open her eyes and meet his. As always, their blueness profoundly unsettled her. "I'm sorry about your boat. And the Caribbean and everything."

He raised one shoulder indifferently. "There are other boats, other oceans. I'll try the East China Sea. Sounds good."

"Yes." *Oh, Connor,* she thought unhappily. *I'll miss you. More than I dare tell you. Don't go away. Stay. I'd ask you to kiss me if only I could. I'd ask you to hold me in your arms again. But I don't know how. I'm afraid.*

I'm afraid I'd love you so much I'd never get over it. I can't stand losing someone again. I can't. You don't know how it hurts.

She feared that all the longing, all the contradictions she felt, were naked in her eyes.

Connor looked at her a long time. But if he read what she thought, he said nothing of it. Instead, he smiled his crooked half smile. "Don't look sad, Gina. It's festival time. It's what you love most. Eat. Drink." He touched his wineglass to hers again. "And be merry."

"I can't be merry," she said, her voice choked. She rose swiftly from the table and fled upstairs to the safety of the guest room.

She lay on the bed, hugging her pillow, her eyes stinging with unshed tears and her heart drumming so hard her head ached with it.

For a few mad moments, she thought he might follow her, make his way up the stairs and confront her, force her to be honest with him. And if he did . . .

She didn't dare finish the thought.

But he didn't come after her. She felt as if she had been exiled, alone, to another planet. Through the window, as if mocking her, came the faint sounds of the festival.

THE REMAINING TWO DAYS of the festival danced by in a bittersweet blur. Gina worked as long and hard as she could, at every job she was asked to do.

Her help was sought when Billy Ray Fenelli split his Elvis pants again. For the second year in a row, she found herself in the little makeshift dressing room, sewing madly.

Although Gina was kept as busy as possible, she still managed to see Earline every visiting hour, and almost wept with relief when the older woman was allowed to come home Sunday morning.

Earline looked full of spunk—just like her old self. *She's going to be fine,* Gina thought. *There isn't any emergency, and I won't have to think of Beekman at all. I can put him out of my mind. We're safe again.*

Connor volunteered to take care of Earline while Gina went back to the festival. Gina was grateful he was staying behind. The day before, he'd volunteered to take Wesley Dean to the carnival, the frog-jumping contest and the spaghetti supper.

It had seemed that no matter where Gina went, she unexpectedly encountered Connor, or that Wesley Dean, Connor in tow, was seeking her out and demanding she pay attention to them. They had the bullfrog, Mr. Munroe, with them, and Mr. Munroe had distinguished himself by winning second place in the jumping contest. Connor looked, well, almost proud of both boy and frog.

To make things worse, Connor seemed to be going out of his way to charm the socks off everyone in Allegro. They all kept asking her about him. Gina stayed evasive and hid behind an innocent smile until her jaws hurt from it.

She worked Sunday night until the last supper was served, the last table cleared, the last dish washed. By then, the carnival was pulling up stakes. The rides were being dismantled and put back on their trucks, the booths and stalls knocked down and loaded. The caravan would leave Allegro at dawn.

Shortly after midnight, Gina walked the deserted midway area with Snicky Alonzo, helping him check the grounds. The grass was trampled, the dust unsettled, but the fields, dark again, looked eerily empty. The breeze blew across them, unimpeded. No longer dimmed by carnival lights, the stars shone down, twinkling brightly in the velvet darkness of the sky.

"No need to keep me company, Gina," Snicky said in his creaky voice as they turned back toward the parish hall. He was a small man whose arthritis made him walk slowly. "Go home to Earline. I know you want to."

Gina shrugged and looked up at the hazy sprawl of stars across the sky. "She's fine, Snick. I called every hour. She's asleep and should be till morning."

She took a deep breath of the clean night air. "It was a wonderful festival, wasn't it? The best ever, I think."

"Too big," Snicky muttered, shaking his head. "Last one *I* intend to fool with. Why ain't you goin' home? You scared of that feller?"

Gina's back stiffened and her shoulders tensed. "I'm not scared of anybody. And every year everybody's ready to stop having festival by the time it's over. But give you a week, and you'll all be planning the next one."

Snicky shook his head. "Can't go on forever, Gina. Some of us are gettin' too old for it—me, Earline, Sophia Marchesi, a bunch of us. Now if your young man wants you to sell . . ."

"He's not my young man, Snicky," Gina said unhappily. "And I don't have any plans to sell anything to anybody. As far as I know, things'll keep going on in Allegro the way they always have."

"They ain't, they don't and they won't," Snicky said.

"What?" she asked, puzzled.

"They ain't never gone on the same way. They don't and they won't. Always has been changes, always will be. That's what's life's about, is change. You can't stop it, no matter how hard you try." He paused, then added, "And if he ain't your feller, then why do you get that look on your face when he's about? Ain't seen you look like that for years."

Gina bit her lower lip. "He's not my 'feller.' He's going away tomorrow and he won't be back."

"Then you oughtta go with him," said Snicky. "Do you good. Besides, you could afford to see a bit of the world."

Gina stared at him, shocked. "Go with him? I'd never go with him. Leave Allegro? Allegro's my home."

"Some says," Snicky said archly, "that home is where the heart's at. Now when that feller leaves and you're standin' here in Allegro starin' after him, just where do you think your heart's gonna be? Can you answer me that—and answer me honest?"

But Gina could only look down at the trampled grass and say nothing. If there was an honest answer to Snicky's question, she didn't know what it was.

IN THE MORNING Wesley Dean came over to run and fetch for Earline while Gina drove Connor to the doctor's.

Gina's emotions were so torn she had little to say. Neither did Connor. He wore an expression that seemed half angry, half resigned.

He seemed no happier when the doctor pronounced him in good shape, told him to use his foot but to take it easy for a while. Gina gave a grateful sigh. Having both him and Earline on the invalid list in so short a period had left her drained.

"I'll drive," Connor said when they came out of the clinic.

Gina wanted to ask him if he thought he should, but bit back the question. After all, he would soon be driving out of Allegro altogether. There was no longer any doctor's order to stop him.

He sighed with satisfaction as he turned on the ignition. Then he gritted his teeth and stepped on the gas pedal. Furtively Gina watched his profile as they sped, all too swiftly, back toward Allegro.

She tried conversation only once. "I . . . don't suppose you've talked to Beekman again?"

"No," he said curtly, not looking at her.

"I . . . Now that I know Earline's going to be well, I don't feel as pressured—although the whole thing's been kind of a warning. I've been thinking of giving up my shop and getting a job in Milledgeville. It'd certainly pay more—"

"Why, Gina," he said with a smile so mocking it seemed almost bitter, "is that you talking? Thinking about the future instead of the past?"

She shrugged hopelessly, as if it was useless to try to talk. Everything had, after all, already been said.

He surprised her by taking a left turn instead of a right when they came to the turnoff for Allegro. She looked at him in puzzlement. But he said nothing, the same defiant look on his face. The wind tossed his golden hair and he narrowed his eyes against the sun. Gina pushed a blowing curl out of her eyes and waited for him to explain.

He explained nothing. But when they reached the old road that led to the abandoned cannery, he took it, and the car bucked over its ruts and weedy tussocks.

He pulled up sharply in front of the dilapidated building, parked the car and switched it off. He leaned his elbow on the MG's open window, put his chin on his fist and stared at the factory in disgust. By daylight, the rust and disrepair were far more obvious than by moonlight. The roof seemed to sag even more sadly.

"My God," he said, almost to himself, "it's worse than I remembered."

Gina followed his gaze. "I used to think it was kind of . . . enchanted. I suppose that sounds funny to you."

He shrugged impatiently. "Maybe it is enchanted. Or maybe just full of ghosts and bad luck. I'll see."

Gina lowered one brow in a frown. "You'll see? What do you mean?"

"I mean," Connor said with an expression of intense irritation, "that I bought it. I set out to buy a fleet of yachts, and this is what I get instead. I should have my head examined, dammit."

Her jaw dropped. "Connor! You bought it? Why?"

He shrugged again. "I don't know why. Because it seemed like a good idea at the time. Or maybe so Beekman couldn't buy it. He had his chance. Well, he won't get it again."

Gina could hardly find her voice. "But what will you do with a tomato cannery? You don't want a tomato cannery."

He turned to her, his eyes flashing dangerously. "Don't I? Late that night after I talked to Beekman, I suddenly decided maybe I did want one. For Beekman's sake, I'd convinced myself it was such a good idea that when he said no, I thought I'd show the old geezer."

"That *what's* such a good idea?" Gina demanded, bewildered by his mood.

"A cannery. A cannery in Allegro is a good idea," he said with mock patience. "The sauce can be made right here. With Allegro tomatoes and tomato paste shipped up from Texas. Yeah, I decided it was a great idea, so I bought it. And also that old movie theater in town. I decided that was a good idea, too."

"The movie theater?" Her eyes widened in disbelief. "You want to buy an empty movie theater? In Allegro of all places?"

"No," he said with a short self-mocking laugh. "I want to buy an elephant factory in Allegro. That theater has more square footage than any other empty building in town. It'll do."

"Connor—an *elephant factory?*"

He shook his head at his own folly. "Right. I'm not going to the Caribbean to restore yachts. Or to Korea to play with mills. I'm staying here to manufacture spaghetti sauce. And to go into the toy-elephant business. With Earline's designs.''

''What?'' she cried.

''Look,'' he said with a curt gesture, ''I twisted the truth a little. A guy in the toy business did buy all Earline's elephants. Except he's just starting the business. I'm the guy.''

Speechless, she could only stare at him.

''Look, Gina,'' he said, his face taut, ''it came to me, and I realized it was a Big Idea, the kind that makes the back of your neck go cold. Handmade toys—limited editions of them, patterned after Earline's originals, the kind of stuff sold only in fine stores.''

''But—'' Gina started to protest.

''She only likes to make one of a kind. Fine—that's all she has to do. She makes the prototypes. Then workers make a limited number of faithful copies—maybe a couple of thousand. Who knows how far the thing could go, how it might expand? I could make a lot of money. So could Earline.''

Gina shook her head in disbelief. ''You and Earline have talked about this? When?''

''When you were at your precious festival. We talked—we didn't say anything concrete, because I didn't want to excite her. But we came to an…understanding, you might call it.''

''And you bought all her elephants?''

He nodded, his expression partly humorous, partly scornful. ''Yeah. Me. For prototypes. They're in Wesley's garage.''

''Wesley? Wesley Dean?''

He looked insulted by her surprise. ''Wesley Dean happens to think the world of me. An extremely bright child, Wesley Dean. He and his mother were glad to do a favor for me. Wesley Dean, in fact, very much wants me to stay in

Allegro. He says I can tell the goriest stories he's ever heard.''

Gina put her hand to her mouth and shook her head helplessly, once more unable to speak.

Connor darted her a frown. ''Earline wants me to stay, too. For different reasons, of course. She thinks I might be good for you. In fact, in the last couple of days, several people have taken me aside to say that—that I might be good for you.'' He frowned. ''A lot of people,'' he added almost defiantly.

She stared at him, not certain she had correctly understood.

''Wesley's mother, for one,'' he said defensively. ''Ralph Marchesi, for another. And his aunt Sophia. His daughter Lindy. Even the famous Snicky Alonzo, who made sure to check me out. In fact, almost everybody in town *did* check me out and said it, too—with one notable exception.''

She looked puzzled.

''You,'' he said irritably. ''You've never said I might be good for you. Not with words. Oh, no, never with words. But sometimes in the last few days, I thought I saw it in your eyes. And if I was wrong, I've just made the biggest fool in the world of myself.''

''I don't understand,'' she breathed, her heart starting to beat like the wings of some creature that was quickly taking flight.

He reached for the steering wheel with one hand and gripped it until his knuckles paled. ''That first night of the festival. When you came back from the hospital. You looked at me as if... I don't know, maybe as if you wanted me. Or needed me. Or both. I only knew I couldn't go away. I had to to stay. To see if it was true. The look on your face. And what it said.''

He picked up her left hand. ''What I thought that look said was this....'' Gently he drew Loren's ring from her finger, then turned over her hand, pressing the ring into her palm and closing her fingers over it. But he kept her hand captured in his and stared into her eyes.

"I thought your look said it was time to take this off." He squeezed her hand and all she felt was the electricity of his touch. The ring's weight seemed to vanish, no more solid than a ghost. "I thought you might believe it was finally time to put that ring away, Gina," he said softly. "Was I right?"

He loosened his grasp so that her fingers unfolded. Her hand still lay within his, Loren's ring glinting in her palm.

She stared at it for what seemed an endless moment, her throat tight. "Yes," she almost whispered. "You're right."

With her free hand she took the ring and dropped it into the pocket of her denim skirt. Tremulously, she withdrew her hand, bare and empty, and Connor lifted it to his mouth and kissed it.

"Gina," he said. "Your eyes said you wanted me to stay. Is it true? Or have I been an idiot and bought a cannery and an elephant factory for no good reason?"

She nodded. "No," she answered softly. "Yes. I want you to stay. More than anything."

"Come on," he said, almost smiling. "Let's get out of this fool car. Walk me to the pond. Where you used to sit with your father and watch the red-winged blackbirds."

He got out, went around to her side, opened the door and, taking her hand, drew her out. Slowly they started through the nodding weeds and wildflowers toward the pond. He kept her hand in his.

"If you stay," she said, trying to swallow the lump forming in her throat, "how long would you stay?"

He shook his head, as if he didn't know himself. "How long would you have me?"

Her throat grew more choked and she gripped his hand tighter. "How long *could* you stay? This isn't your kind of place, Allegro. It's not your kind of life, staying in one place...."

The pond glinted bright silver in the morning light, and a blue kingfisher flew away as Connor and Gina approached the water's edge. Connor paused, taking both Gina's hands in his.

"I realized," he said slowly, "that I wanted Mercator's yacht for one reason. It was the one place in the world I ever remembered feeling at home, feeling I belonged. It was the only place I'd ever allowed myself to have ties to."

He shook his head, looking away from her a moment, past the bright glitter of the pond. "All my life I'd wanted to belong somewhere," he said from between his teeth. "I envied kids who did. I envied them like crazy. Once, I finally felt like I belonged—but only on *The Solitaire*. But then that time was over—and it hurt. So I made believe it didn't and made believe I liked being alone, not having any roots, not wanting any."

He turned to face her again. "I suppose I thought if I got *The Solitaire* back, I'd get the old feelings back. That urge was only a sign—a sign that I was ready to find home. I just didn't know where. Or understand home isn't so much a place as it's people. It's... loving."

"Oh, Connor," she said, slipping her hands up to his shoulders, happy to grip their solidity, happy to know he was truly there, saying such things to her.

He slid his hands to her waist, spanning it, drawing her nearer. "I never wanted to love a place, Gina. Or a person. I never wanted to be that vulnerable. But I fell in love with Allegro because you made me see it through your eyes. And I fell in love with you because... because how could I help it?"

"Oh, Connor," she said, standing on tiptoe, raising her lips to his. "Would you kiss me? Would you hold me? Please, oh, please?"

"Gina... you asked," he said raggedly, as her mouth brushed his. Then he crushed her in his arms and kissed her, and kissed her again, and kept kissing her until they were both breathless.

They held each other tightly and she buried her face against his shoulder. He stroked her back, caressing her.

"I never tried to start a business before," he said against her hair. "I always took crippled ones and tried to prop them back up. I didn't want anything I'd get too involved with. Now I'm trying to start two, and I'm involved up to my neck. I want to save your town for you, Gina. I don't know if I can. I'm not Superman. But we'll see. You're right—it's a way of life that shouldn't die. Somebody's got to try to save it. We'll see."

She smiled up at him, giddy with love. "You can do anything."

He smiled back crookedly. "Maybe. And maybe you can help me solve the problem that bothered me most with Beekman."

"What?" she asked, losing herself in his eyes.

He laid a forefinger against one of her dimples. "I hated that you might have had to sell the recipe when you didn't want to. Now you don't. Just marry me—then it stays in the family. Want to get married and go into the spaghetti business? Oh, you'll have to go to the Caribbean with me now and then, or the East China Sea. But this will be home. For both of us, if you'll just say so. If you say yes, I'll tie this cannery up in a pink bow again, for you, on our wedding day. What do you think?"

She smiled more widely, because she knew he was outrageous enough to do it. "I think we can have a long, happy and very spicy future," she said.

He kissed her first on her left dimple. "Very long," he murmured. Then on the right. "Very happy."

Then, smiling, he took her face between his hands and drank in the happiness shining out of her eyes. "And very, very spicy," he breathed, lowering his lips to hers.

Earline's Brownies

Brownies:

2 cups granulated sugar
2 cups flour
¼ cup cocoa
1 cup water
¼ lb margarine
½ cup vegetable oil
1 tsp baking soda
½ cup buttermilk
2 eggs
½ cup chopped pecans

Frosting:

¼ cup cocoa
¼ lb margarine
⅓ cup buttermilk
1 lb box powdered sugar
1 tsp vanilla
½ cup chopped pecans

1. Preheat oven to 350°
2. Sift 2 cups sugar, 2 cups flour, ¼ cup cocoa into a large bowl. Set aside.
3. Bring 1 cup water, ¼ lb margarine and ½ cup of vegetable oil to a boil. Stir to keep from scorching. Add to dry ingredients from step two. Set aside.
4. Beat together 1 tsp baking soda, ½ cup buttermilk, 2 eggs and add to bowl from step three.
5. Add ½ cup of chopped pecans to mixture. Stir and then pour into 12″ × 18″ pan. Bake 20-22 minutes.

Frosting: Begin frosting so it will be ready the minute the brownies come out of the oven.

1. Bring ¼ cup cocoa, ¼ lb margarine, ⅓ cup buttermilk to a boil.
2. Add 1 box of powdered sugar, 1 tsp vanilla to mixture. Stir or beat until smooth.
3. Add ½ cup of chopped pecans to frosting. Stir and then spread on HOT brownies. Let stand 12 hours. Enjoy!

HARLEQUIN ROMANCE®

**brings you the
exciting conclusion of**

THE BRIDAL COLLECTION

next month with

THE REAL McCOY
by Patricia Knoll

THE BRIDE ran away.
THE GROOM ran after her.
THEIR MARRIAGE was over. *Or was it?*

Available this month in
The Bridal Collection
TEMPORARY ARRANGEMENT
by Shannon Waverly
Harlequin Romance #3259

Wherever Harlequin books are sold.

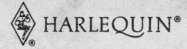

THE TAGGARTS OF TEXAS!

Harlequin's Ruth Jean Dale brings you
THE TAGGARTS OF TEXAS!

Those Taggart men—strong, sexy and hard to resist...

You've met Jesse James Taggart in FIREWORKS!
Harlequin Romance #3205 (July 1992)

And Trey Smith—he's THE RED-BLOODED YANKEE!
Harlequin Temptation #413 (October 1992)

And the unforgettable Daniel Boone Taggart in SHOWDOWN!
Harlequin Romance #3242 (January 1993)

Now meet Boone Smith and the Taggarts who started it all—
in LEGEND!
Harlequin Historical #168 (April 1993)

Read all the Taggart romances!
Meet all the Taggart men!

Available wherever Harlequin Books are sold.

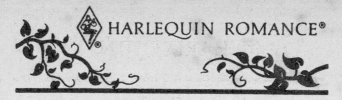

HARLEQUIN ROMANCE®

welcomes you

BACK TO THE RANCH

Let your favorite Romance authors take you West!

Authors like Susan Fox, Debbie Macomber, Roz Denny, Rebecca Winters and more!

Let them introduce you to wonderful women and strong, sexy men—the men of the West. Ranchers and horsemen and cowboys and lawmen...

Beginning in June 1993

Wherever Harlequin books are sold.